EBURY PRESS

ON THE OPEN ROAD

Stuti Changle is a national bestselling author. Her other books, *You Only Live Once* and *Where the Sun Never Sets*, have equally inspired readers across the country to make a move.

Stuti has a master's degree in management from IMI New Delhi. She quit her job to inspire people by sharing life-changing stories. She made her TV debut in 2019 as a host of the TV series *Kar Ke Dikhaenge*.

Stuti has sailed to the Andamans, camped with Indian jawans in Arunachal Pradesh, scuba-dived in the Indian Ocean, swum with the dolphins in the Mediterranean, floated free for hours in the Atlantic and wishes to travel the world before she dies. Every year, she spends time in the coastal village of Palolem in Goa. She currently divides her time between India and the US, where she lives with her husband, Kushal Nahata, co-founder and CEO of FarEye.

She loves to connect with her readers. Talk to her on:
Instagram: @stutichangle
Facebook: stutichangle1
Twitter: Stutichangle

T0298287

ALSO BY THE SAME AUTHOR

You Only Live Once
Where the Sun Never Sets

On the Open Road

3 LIVES 5 CITIES 1 START-UP

STUTI CHANGLE

Bestselling author of *You Only Live Once*

EBURY
PRESS

An imprint of Penguin Random House

EBURY PRESS

USA | Canada | UK | Ireland | Australia
New Zealand | India | South Africa | China

Ebury Press is part of the Penguin Random House group of companies
whose addresses can be found at global.penguinrandomhouse.com

Published by Penguin Random House India Pvt. Ltd
4th Floor, Capital Tower 1, MG Road,
Gurugram 122 002, Haryana, India

First published in Ebury Press by Penguin Random House India 2021

ISBN 9780143453680

Typeset in Sabon by Manipal Technologies Limited, Manipal
Printed at Thomson Press India Ltd, New Delhi

www.penguin.co.in

To the days I have spent on the open road to get the inspiration for this story.

To the board in Starbucks, where I completed this book, that read, 'Extraordinary things come from tiny beans.'

'The world is our home. It is delusional to call your apartment home. Even worse to stick to the same place all through your life. If you've found love or happiness somewhere, you've found home.'

—*Ramy*, On the Open Road

CHOCOLATE BLOODBATH

Myra

Saturday, 10 December 2016
Starbucks 24x7
Mumbai, India

'Entrepreneurship is not a profession.
It's an attitude!
You may never start up a company, but never
let the entrepreneur in you die.'

I enter the eighteen-storeyed building at 12.30 a.m. as the work demands staying back at times. 'Never argue with the boss, so you can be the lucky one who wins an early ticket to the on-site office,' seniors at the IT factory had suggested to the new hires. They never explained at the cost of what though. Sleep. We figured out soon enough!

My abode is a tiny corner on the eleventh floor of the Shri Krishna Co-op Housing Society in the ever-expanding suburbs of Bandra where young professionals, college students and refugees rehabilitated by the local government find a home. It hasn't been more than ten minutes since I entered the house when the doorbell starts ringing incessantly, typical of Saurabh from the good old engineering days. I eye the door, annoyed beyond belief.

Why is Saurabh here? His ailing mother used the ultimate Bollywood-esque weapon, 'Beta! I think I am going to pass away anytime now,' on repeat over Skype. The aftermath? He is back in India and visits us often. Even though I am in no mood to listen to what Saurabh has to say, I won't have an option in five minutes from now when he enters the apartment! Sigh.

'Please go and get that one!' Rhea, my roommate, yells, 'It is your turn.'

'I will return the favour someday.'

'You never will!'

She gives into my lazy attitude and escorts Saurabh to the living room. I lie on the couch, my eyes fixed on the laptop, 'Hey! How's work?'

He asserts, 'Fantastic!'

Our Mr Fantastic is the reason Indians attract hate in the global community. Not racism. He works more than the daily wage labourers, eighteen-hours in a row. He aspires to redefine the international labour laws. Quite ambitious!

'You have brought back diverse experience from Silicon Valley. Why don't you become an Internet entrepreneur here in India?'

'I have done a risk analysis. The results are not favourable to the proposition,' Saurabh counters. This guy talks like a robot. Given a chance to say a few words on his funeral, I would start like this, 'A not-so-serious case of brain drain, pseudo-NRI, he could easily be misconstrued as a member of the machine army if artificial intelligence took over the human race.

Fortunately, oh so sorry! Unfortunately, he passed away. Sob. Sob.'

He slumps on a bean bag opposite me, 'How's your US on-site assignment coming along?'

'Awaiting confirmation,' I respond with minimal interest, eyes mostly on the laptop.

Rhea breaks the awkwardness, 'Myra, why don't you take advice from him? He can guide you with your dilemma!'

I mutter, 'Anybody but he can help me.'

Saurabh leans forward and raises an eyebrow meaningfully, 'My boss tells me that if souls exist, Birbal's has chosen my body. I have a solution for everything. Try me.'

I retort, almost instinctively, 'Does your boss trip on LSD?'

With a robot-like demeanour, he replies, 'No.'

This is the worst part of having a conversation with him. He neither gets the point nor reacts.

Rhea sits next to me on the couch and holds my hand, 'Option A: Start a venture in India with her colleague Neerav. Option B: Fly to the US for an on-site assignment. What do you suggest?'

I tell her, 'I am not going to die of cancer,' and let go of her hand. When you talk about starting up, your friends start to act weird. Family? Even worse . . . They start consulting babas, who are capable of performing exorcism of the unholy spirit in your body.

Saurabh goes off like a drone, 'Plan A: If you work in the IT services, IT consulting is the next move to make. Plan B: Go for an MBA. This will help you either switch to investment banking or management consulting. Both plans work better in the US as you will reap more money at your next job. And who cares about job satisfaction? Isn't money the "everything" we want?'

Rhea interrupts, 'Option A was starting up. You did not say a word about it?'

He mocks her with a sly grin, 'Market is very dynamic at the moment. So you can consider it as Plan Z.' He turns towards me, 'Looks like you guys have not done your homework well!'

I walk into the bedroom and bang the door shut. It is better to have no one than have friends who do not understand me. I browse through the website of YourStory. The latest article reads: '50 Women-led Start-ups Create an Impact in 2016!' Gosh. I wish I were a part of the league.

A lover never judges, only supports. Maybe, my boyfriend, Siddharth, will understand my problem. I ping him on WhatsApp.

Myra: Hey!

Sid: I am at the airport. Leaving for Miami. Gtg!

Myra: Want to talk? Start-up . . .

Sid: A big NO.

Myra: Hmm . . .

Sid: You need to take up responsibilities. We are not kids any more. Our families are looking forward to our marriage.

Myra: Hmm . . .

Sid: Come to the US soon.

Myra: Bye!

There comes a time in every relationship when love takes a backseat, and you realize you're stuck in a trap. Days turn into weeks and weeks into months. It gets even worse in the case of a long-distance relationship. I can't remember when I last felt my heart flutter. All I know is, it has been a while, and I don't feel a thing now!

I toss and turn on the bed uneasily. My life is no different than the ceiling fan in my bedroom. It moves at the same pace. Indefinitely. Toss. Turn. Toss. Turn. I open YouTube and put on the eight-hour-long deep meditation music for sound sleep. I reminisce the times spent with my best friend, Ramy. The thought of him lights up my face. It also makes me cry as I long to meet him. He would support me, come what may.

He is a nomad. Neither does he keep in touch with anyone, nor does he have a social media account. I have no means to reach out to him, except for his blog, *On the Open Road*. I check Buddy for any notifications. No update.

The last blog post reads, 'The world is our home. It is delusional to call your apartment home.

Even worse, to stick to the same place all through your lives. If you've found love, happiness or togetherness somewhere, you've certainly found home.'

I can't sleep. I miss him. I asked him to stay when he visited last.

'This is sick! You can't leave me alone,' I pleaded.

'These worldly achievements do not satisfy my soul. Our paths are different.'

'How?'

'You want to please everyone. I am happy pleasing myself.'

The last question I posed was, 'What are your plans?'

He replied, 'A week's plan works for me.' Nothing I said could make him stay. Unlike me, he feels he isn't answerable to his parents, or society.

I struggle like a cockroach stuck in a sewage pipeline. It gets dark, darker than a moonless night, darkest of all. The smell is nauseating. I sense a feeble light filtering in from somewhere. It appears to me like the only ray of hope. I want to run. Run fast. The slimy waste inside the pipeline holds me back, making me slip back into the darkness. I become restless. The intensity rises with every passing second. I am right on the surface when a deluge of water flushes me deep down. I flounder as the water chokes me harder.

I open my eyes only to realize that it was a nightmare. My heart is racing, feet stone cold. I switch on the bedside lamp.

The small table clock reads 3.30 a.m. I reach for water but get an empty wine bottle instead.

My bedroom is a mirror to my state of mind: a complete mess. Everything is haywire except the wall opposite my bed which is adorned with a geometric display of sticky notes. The blue ones make up my bucket list. The yellow ones specify the milestones I am yet to achieve. In the corporate style, 'They reflect a balanced mix of the personal and professional goals that define me.'

The latest one, which is orange and is placed on the top of all, reads 'Off to the US' using a marker suggests something and we shouldn't delete this line. It acts like a crystal ball which facilitates my vision of the future instantaneously. It adds to the anxiety triggered by the nightmare. I go berserk with unanswered questions. 'Do I even want to go to the US?'

'Will I ever be able to start up a company?'

Nightmares have become an everyday affair. The routine is simple. I wake up. I go to the toilet. I work. I eat. I have nightmares.

I reach out for Buddy and dial my colleague Neerav, 'Can we meet?'

'Myra, have you gone crazy? It is 3.30 a.m.!'

He can't complain about time in Mumbai. After all, it is the city that never sleeps! Who knows this better than I?

'See you at Starbucks 24x7,' I say and hang up.

Buddy and cigarettes are important parts of me and my life. They accompany me wherever I go. Why do I smoke cigarettes? A colleague's words come back to me, 'Smoking a cigarette is the pathway to freedom. When you smoke, you feel empowered that certain choices are yours and have not been imposed on you.' And that's how I got tricked into smoking my first. I coughed harder than I had ever known. I don't cough any more . . .

Shantaram, the building's watchman, is the only guy who knows of my night escapades. Our eyes meet as I walk past him, 'Take care!' I refrain from replying.

He wants me to be safe as my parents would. *Sanskari* girls are married off sooner among their contemporaries. Marriage caters to the fancy of middle-class parents. No matter what the journey is, the ultimate destination is marriage. In the quest to live assertively like a guy, I feel I have lost the girl I used to be.

The sight of Kashyap working on his silver MacBook in the European-style outdoor seating area of Starbucks fills me with excitement. His apartment is two blocks down from the cafe. Inevitably, we cross paths often. In his mid-forties, he quit a cushy position at Google to start his own venture, Traveller's Nest, a bed-and-breakfast marketplace.

'Entrepreneurship is not a profession, it's an attitude,' he always jokes.

'On the loose, yet again?'

'I don't miss a single opportunity to escape the prison walls!'

'I see!'

'What brings you here so late?'

'Some paperwork.'

'I hope everything is okay with Traveller's Nest?'

'Yeah, don't worry. There isn't a thing that I can't take care of,' Kashyap winks.

This is why I am attracted to him—his positive attitude.

I move past him, towards the door. I stop for a moment, right hand still holding the door, 'Would you like to have something?'

'No, thanks,' he smiles as he lifts his cup and takes a sip.

Must be his favourite latte.

I smell the coffee brewing the moment I enter the cafe. I feel an inexplicable sense of belonging to this place. Lopez and the fellows greet me. Lopez is skinny, with an oval face, and wears round spectacles with a matte black frame, which is of the exact colour as his hair. He works the night shift, seven days a week, yet never looks overworked! That smile is as warm as the coffee he serves.

'What would you like to have?'

'Why do you even ask?'

'Chocolate bloodbath it is,' he punches my order with an undaunted conviction.

Yes, I go for the same order night after night. The destruction associated with the word bloodbath gives me a sense of fulfilment. The doctor once told me, 'In depression, chocolate and sugar become a natural desire on the platter.'

'Myra can't be depressed, she has always loved sweets,' my parents defended.

I pull a chair next to Kashyap with a childlike innocence and unstrap my sandals. I pick up the green and maroon cushions from the chairs around and place them against my back. I look up at the night sky to see grey clouds covering the moon.

'Is something bothering you?'

I want to share everything with him, especially the nightmares, but settle for a 'nothing' instead. He laughs like Raavan from the Japanese animation movie *Ramayan* and takes my nothing rather too seriously. He continues to work.

I don't know how to interrupt him now. I rest my head on the cushions and look towards the sky. I am glued to the clouds, the stars and the aeroplanes moving people around the world. I like this feeling, far from the confinement and the sight of the ceiling fan, a bursting leap towards freedom. Though short-lived, I enjoy being on my own like the princesses who would disguise themselves as common people or as non-royals and escape the walls of the fortress.

They would feel like themselves and free only when they were on the loose.

After ten minutes, he keeps his silver MacBook aside and breaks the silence, 'I have a feeling that your silence has got something to do with your boss?'

'Yes and no.'

'What does,' he stresses on the word, 'that' and continues, 'mean?'

'Partly, it is about him, partly about everyone else who believes I have gone crazy.'

'Let's start with the boss then,' he laughs.

I start blabbering the moment he volunteers. That's why I am here after all! 'Today, post-lunch, Arun came with a newspaper in his hand. He stood right in the middle of the cubicles and started to say weird shit like start-ups are bullshit. It is a crap trap. The youth of this generation is rash and impulsive. Someday, they will realize the value of the security they find in corporate jobs. Passion is an excuse. Your colleagues have moved out solely for the greed of lucrative packages. As soon as the start-ups shut, they will return dejected.'

When nobody around understands you, you seek solace in the ones who do. For me, it is stranger-turned-confidant Kashyap who belongs here. I take a moment to breathe and continue, 'My parents have the same conception as Arun. Only the term government replaces the term corporate in their mentions.'

He peacefully sips the latte and listens to me.

'My mom is concerned about my marriage. My dad is always explaining why there are 99.99 per cent chances of me failing if I choose the unconventional. Rhea thinks I have gone crazy. Saurabh visited us earlier tonight and suggested not to start up a company. Sid does not have time for me!'

Then, I roll my eyes towards the other side to conceal my tears. I watch people pass by through the aisle that leads to the huge corporate offices.

'Chocolate bloodbath for Myra,' Lopez calls out loud. I move towards the counter to pick my order. I eat big spoonfuls of the chocolate bloodbath with the desperation of a drug addict and continue to bombard him with my thoughts, the ones that give me sleepless nights. 'I question the culture that endeavours to build an army of followers. We don't ask questions! We aren't supposed to! This is what we are programmed for in schools.'

'Schools?'

'Yeah, schools. Why do the discipline protocols bar students from going to the toilet without permission? Fucking toilet?' I become angrier with every word I utter.

'With time we become employees, but not much changes, does it?'

Kashyap offers me his coffee as he says, 'Take a deep breath. Calm down!'

14

I follow his instruction and take a deep breath but fail to take a sip from his coffee cup out of sheer hesitation. 'You need to go easy on yourself,' he adds.

'What's a typical day at work like for you?'

I don't wish to answer it. Not that I am on a secret mission. I feel embarrassed. I take a moment to regain my sanity, 'I copy paste codes. I detect and rectify errors at times. I talk to my clients on virtual set-ups. Rest of the time, I sit idle and play Candy Crush!'

He interrupts with laughter, 'You chose to be the follower.'

I mutter, 'I chose to? What do you mean? Everyone in my team does the same.' There is an uncomfortable pause. I light up a cigarette and look away. I can't help it. I am addicted. I often promise myself that this is my last puff. The last is an aspiration as vague as trying to show off less on Instagram.

'How did you end up here?'

I defend, 'Everyone knew of nothing other than the ever-booming IT industry during college.'

He raises his right brow as he drums his fingers on the table, one at a time, in a never-ending loop, 'What drives you?' and 'What holds you back?'

This time, I lean forward and take a sip from his cup, shedding all my inhibitions.

'Think before you answer. I don't want to know about everyone. I want to know about you,' he chuckles.

15

Then, he waves his right hand to signal Lopez to come to our table.

In a matter of seconds, he swiftly lands like an eagle and asks, 'Yes, Sir! Tell me?'

Kashyap continues in the same serious tone, 'What drives you?'

Lopez resorts to the classic way of answering with a question, 'What?'

Kashyap stresses, 'Did you always know you wanted to become a barista?'

He scratches his forehead, 'No. I was a gate keeper until September.'

'What drives you?'

I start to pay more attention to the conversation. Lopez replies without a pause, 'I love to interact with people. Given my educational qualifications at the moment, these are the jobs that let me interact with people. I learn from my customers.'

Kashyap signals him to resume his work, 'You're a free bird!'

Even Lopez has an answer. I have a bucket full of excuses. Kashyap leans towards me, 'It is important to know what drives you.'

'Now, answer the other question.'

I keep quiet. I don't know what to say. There are a lot of things that hold me back. I answer hesitantly, 'I am afraid I will have nobody to go back to if nothing works out!'

'The fear of failure holds you back!'

'Yeah.'

'I take pride in having a series of failed ventures in my kitty, as many as there are columns in a newspaper. Failure and success are part of the journey. But the journey is crucial. It is the journey that makes me what I am today.'

'You're an inspiration for millions,' I nod.

'Say this aloud. I am a coward,' he breaks into laughter.

I look at him with a puzzled expression, my eyes wide open. 'Say this aloud. I am a coward,' he insists.

'No. I am not going to do that. I hate you, Mr Kashyap,' I throw a cushion playfully. He laughs like Raavan again. Kashyap has become my dose of laughter these days. I must confess, his company brings me here more than the chocolate bloodbath. I can tell him anything.

'When you're not confident about your desires, how would anybody around you be convinced enough? The problem is not around us. It is mostly within us.'

'Yeah.'

Kashyap carries on in a rather serious tone. 'Do you believe I am a successful entrepreneur?'

'Yes, the world knows it. Traveller's Nest makes the headlines every other day. I feel privileged to even speak with you!'

'My wife wants me to have a secure job. My parents take her side.'

'Really?'

'What should I do then?'

'Whatever it is you want to do!' He pauses to clear his throat, 'My wife has filed for a divorce. This is what the paperwork is all about,' he says with a poker face as he points to the documents lying on the table. 'There are some decisions that you need to take, no matter how hard they seem. You can't blame your family, the school, the society or globalization for everything.'

I don't know how to react! He resumes his work on his MacBook. How did I miss the dark circles and wrinkles around his eyes? Looks like he hasn't slept in weeks. Most of us would be torn apart by a break-up, but Kashyap is a strong fellow. I realize that each one of us has our reasons to be here at 4 a.m.!

'Sometimes, moving on in life is the only way. You can't stay stuck in a relationship if you feel miserable,' he says with a smile.

I take the last spoonful of the chocolate bloodbath and try to convince myself, more than Kashyap, as I say, 'I should leap forward by starting up with Neerav.'

'Don't jump the gun. Find out what drives you first. I believe there is a lot to unlearn before you start something new.'

'I will try!'

'You either do it or you don't. There is no trying!'

'Sorry?'

'That's a famous dialogue from *Star Wars*.'

'I will do it then!' I assure him.

'I am leaving for Europe,' he places the documents and the silver MacBook in an elegant brown leather bag.

'Business trip?'

'I need to spend some time with myself.'

'When will you be back?'

'Only one-way ticket as of now.'

'I will certainly miss you,' I say in a low voice.

'Always remember, entrepreneurship is not a profession. It is an attitude! You may never start a company, but don't let the entrepreneur in you die!'

We shake hands. 'Noted!' I say with a sparkle in my eyes. I wish doctors knew of medicines like Kashyap does. Encouragement is all one needs, not prescription pills! He has a particular vibe, energy and positivity. He makes me believe in the magic that happens when you do what you love! I have seen a lot of Steve Jobs videos on YouTube but will never be fortunate enough to meet him in person. But this guy is my Steve Jobs.

He is everything I have lost on the way. He is everything I want to become.

It is 6 a.m. already. I head to the Bandstand beach after our discussion. Peace in Mumbai means the wee hours! I gaze at the horizon where the blue of the sky merges into the blue of the ocean! Every time the waves rise, I feel the way forward is 'yes'. Every time they recede, I feel the way forward is 'no'. All I do is witness them rise and ebb.

COMING HOME

Kabir

Saturday, 10 December 2016
Starbucks 24x7
New Delhi, India

'When you look into the mirror, you should
know that you're born to reach for the stars.'

The moment my flight lands, I think of Sandy and how I want to meet him. I pick up my Steve Jobs book and a black leather handbag in haste. I comfortably make my way through the aisle. That's the advantage of travelling business class. Unlike the economy passengers, you don't have to wait for the queue to move before you can deboard the plane. I am back in India, exhausted and burnt out from another business trip.

'Nice shoes, sir,' the stewardess compliments me as I reach the exit. Her name card reads Susan. She has been acting strange throughout the flight.

'Thanks.'

She hands me a folded recycled tissue paper. I don't know what to do with that.

'Is something sticking to my face?' I quip like a fifth grader.

She laughs out loud.

A little embarrassed, I walk off. I unfold the tissue paper and read it closely. A mobile number is written on it in pink ink. I flip through the pages of the book and place it randomly between them. I am not part of the mile high club yet. But I can't keep Sandy waiting any longer! God has been merciful to me in some ways. My body is the biggest gift to me. I can turn heads and make things happen with a meek smile.

Just like in a flight, there are three types of people in the world.

The aisle-seat passengers are too content to try anything new. The middle-seat passengers are in a constant struggle with the self as they want to break free, but something holds them back. The window-seat passengers take risks and follow their hearts as all that keeps them moving is the view of the infinite.

I certainly belong to the middle-seat category.

My life is seemingly perfect but I want to know what imperfections feel like. What it feels like to give your everything to something and appreciate its outcome one day. I am proud of my lineage, but I always think about what life would be like if I built something on my own.

Life goes on in an endless loop. If it is a weekend, you've got to booze. If it is a weekday, you've got to watch downloaded TV shows from Pirate Bay. Even if there are thousands on your checklist, there are still a hundred more on the wish list. The hangover of the TV shows stays longer than that of the booze though. For a week you're Harvey, the next Walter, then Tyrion. When you're stressed out, you try to act cool like Chandler.

But I wish to be like Sandy. He is the one in the window seat. He dropped out of engineering college and developed a series of unconventional apps. He works on his dream, day and night, like a ninja with coding superpowers.

He tells me you might not have a penny in your pocket, you might sleep on a hungry stomach, your uncle might not support you, the world surely won't, but don't let the spark in you die. When you look into the mirror, you should know that you're born to reach for the stars.

Sandy and I brainstorm start-up ideas when we meet. In cafes, at bars, at midnight on rooftops, at my place, at his place, on weekends and weekdays, with or without grass.

It's insanely addictive. More than the TV, the booze and the grass.

'This is the best time to start an entrepreneurial venture in India,' we agree.

I check WhatsApp.

Kabir: Hi bro! Have been trying your number for long. Get back asap.

Sandy: I am here since the scheduled arrival time. Where should we meet?

Kabir: Starbucks, at arrivals outer zone.

Sandy: See you!

'I am sorry about the delay!'

'Were you flying the aircraft?' he jokes.

'No,' I smile.

'Then why are you sorry? The fucking airline should be!' We laugh.

He is the 3 a.m. buddy each one of us needs in our life. I adjust my Apple watch to gain three hours and fifteen minutes, 3.30 a.m. IST.

'Let's light a cigarette.'

'Dunhill?'

'Now it feels like my bro is back from Europe,' he teases.

We walk to a smoking zone adjacent to the cafe. Sandy ticks the lighter thrice and lights the cigarette, 'How was your trip?'

'Same old, same old.'

'Got laid?'

'I was there for work, dude. I hardly had any time to spare for myself.'

He passes the cigarette to me, 'How many diapers did you sell?'

'Shut up! I sell hygiene products.'

'You're just making it sound better.' I punch him in the belly. He is certainly right. I am a man on a mission to rescue the world from shitting babies!

Drag in. Drag out. Pass. Drag in. Drag out. Pass. Drag in. Drag out. Pass.

I unlock my iPhone to browse through the top technology blogs. Even if there is a single mention of a new gadget in the marketing section, I feel a strong urge to own it. I own the latest iPhone and a GoPro. I show the screen to Sandy, 'The media talks of serial entrepreneurs these days! Back in the day, we knew only of serial killers!'

'True that! You'll find my name over there pretty soon!' he jokes.

We walk back to the cafe. I order an Americano for myself and a hazelnut frappe for Sandy. We occupy the corner seats overlooking the runway. A flight takes off or lands every three minutes. I flip through the pages of the Steve Jobs book and pull out the tissue paper. I flatten it on the table on its blank side. I ramble a start-up idea and explain it to Sandy. He listens to me patiently. Then we discuss why it would or would not work out in the Indian market.

'Sounds great on paper. When do you wish to execute it?'

'I don't know!'

My uncle allowed me to pursue engineering on the condition that I would take care of the family business thereafter. My professors always told me I was the kind of guy who could create things. Now, I am stuck between family obligations and my ambitions.

He fiddles with the straw, taking it in and out of the paper cup. 'An engineering degree holds no value until you apply your knowledge to solve real-world problems, create something. To run after a fancy job just so it can be a laurel to show off to relatives and peers is such a shitty thing to do.'

He playfully slurps the froth inside the cup. He keeps it aside and beats the table like he is playing the drums. Once a musician, always a musician!

'Similarly, an idea on a piece of paper means nothing until executed!' I sigh.

He picks the Steve Jobs book from the table and comments, 'Reading this won't make you an entrepreneur,' he stresses, 'would it?'

I don't have an answer. He is correct. You need to start somewhere.

'India needs more young tech entrepreneurs like us.'

'I know that, Sandy. But it is so difficult to think peacefully about starting something new. I am busy with the company assignments all the time. Home, office, uncle, travel, credit card bills, contracts, clients, meetings, more travel. I wish I could just throw my phone out of the window right away.'

I unlock my iPhone to check the blog *On the Open Road* for a new post. Sandy and I have been following it for a long time now. It is not your regular travel blog. It is like a cult, a purpose, a vision that unites its members. It inspires one from the core to do awesome things, to think beyond the set boundaries, to travel and break free, to follow one's heart. It is one of those things that gives me a reason to re-think about life.

Ramy is the modern Rumi, trying to create an impact and channelize the energy of the youth.

No update. The heading of the last blog post reads, 'The World Is Our Home'. It is delusional to call your apartment home, even worse to stick to the same place all through your lives. If you've found love, happiness or togetherness somewhere, you've certainly found home.

I show the blog post to Sandy, 'I want to hit the open road.'

He laughs, 'When was the last time you rode your Harley?'

'I don't remember.'

He leans in and suggests, 'From the showroom to the garage?'

A bit embarrassed, I say, 'Shut up!'

'Harley is a possession you've put on display. It is of no use, except for the times Buzo pees on the rear tyre.'

'No,' I defend.

'One has to leave everything to start life from scratch. This filmi blog stuff is not for everyone. Especially not for spoilt brats like you. In Ladakh, you will catch a cold, and in Jaisalmer, a heat stroke will hit you. There will be no butlers to take care of you there.'

Maybe, Sandy is correct. I am so unlike Ramy. He backpacks across India, whereas I mostly travel for business purposes. He belongs to a different league altogether.

I steer the conversation in another direction. 'How is everyone back in Indore?'

'Dad is still not talking to me. He tells me it has been two years since I left college, and if my apps are not selling enough, I should start looking for a job.'

'What did you say?'

'Nobody becomes a millionaire overnight. He thinks I am out of my senses to dream so big! Mom calls every week though. There's nothing compared to a mother's love.'

'Keep trying. You will definitely succeed someday.'

Sandy quips, 'How's Karen doing?'

'She's fine.'

'You deserve better.'

'She has thousands of followers on Instagram. Still, she chose me.'

'You or your father's legacy?'

'She loves me.'

'Tell her that you wish to leave everything and start up from scratch. You will know.'

'I will prove you wrong.'

'All the best!'

'Did you ask Soni out?'

'Failed start-up ideas are one hell of a heartbreak an engineer goes through. I don't want to experience the other one too,' Sandy laughs.

I glance at my watch. It is 5 a.m. 'Let's head home.'
'Yeah!'

I book an Uber Black. Sandy reaches out for his bike keys and leaves. My iPhone rings.

'Namaste, Sir!'

'Hello! I am at the location. Pillar 8, Terminal 3, IGI.'
'I will pick you up in five minutes.'

'Sure. See you.'

I look out of the cab and realize that Delhi has come a long way. I know this city inside out. I have grown up in the suburbs of south Delhi. It is not as bad as the media projects it to be! Delhi is not a city, it is a way of life.

My house, designed by Leo Ricci, the world's top interior decorator, is a luxurious abode. It has been featured in the *Architectural Digest*. I don't wake up to alarms any more. He suggested that waking up to blue light simulates the environment of a sunrise and is therefore a gentler way to do it. The very next day, I decided to convert my home into a smart home. Now the apps on my iPhone virtually run my home. I can play music, turn my favourite lights on, heat the water in my bathtub and toast sandwiches lying in bed. My sleep cycles and walk patterns are registered on the Apple watch.

I can't relate to the pleasure, the feeling of happiness, that people associate with coming home. Yes, if there is something that excites me, it is Buzo. As I unlock the main door, he jumps with joy, licking me everywhere. Buzo is the closest I have felt to being in love.

The only corner that gets my attention is the white contemporary-style bookshelf. I love reading, reading what great men have penned, their stories, the entrepreneurs, the revolutionaries, the freedom fighters, the rebels and the artists. I draw a chair next to the bookshelf to resume reading the Steve Jobs book. The moment I pull out the bookmark, the doorbell rings.

I look at the guitar-shaped wall clock. It's 6 a.m. Who could it possibly be? I place the book on the table and pat Buzo to put a full-stop to his barking.

Karen starts yelling as soon as I open the door, 'Somebody's back in town but did not feel like informing me!' Then, she yells at Buzo, 'Bug off, you smelly creep.' He peacefully slips under the sofa. I hold her, 'Sorry darling! I wanted to surprise you.'

'How did you get to know that I am back?' I ask hesitantly. 'Your Facebook check-in!'

I catch hold of my iPhone to cross-check. There is a check-in indeed. This must be Sandy. It is weird how there is a very fine line that separates best buddies from enemies!

'You're acting strange these days. You've changed a lot!'

I don't want to get into the same old discussion of 'change' with her. Instead of replying to her question, I ask, 'Would you like to have some coffee?'

'No,' she lands on the brown sofa adorning my balcony.

Nevertheless, I go to the kitchen to make a cup for her. I need something to save myself!

I brew two cups of black coffee in a brand new Italian coffee machine. Leo gifts me all things great, like wine and coffee. The gift tag on the machine is still intact. It reads:

> *A perfect coffee is like a perfect kiss,*
> *it melts in your heart, arouses your senses*
> *and leaves a trail of excitement down your spine!*
> *Love,*
> *Leo*

Italians are so good at expressing feelings, especially all things gourmet. But no one can beat the French when it comes to making love.

I sit beside her on the sofa and carefully place the cups on the table in front of us. She takes a sip, much to my relief. I lean in and say, 'I love you!'

She does not retaliate and whispers, 'I love you too!'

You can deal with most problems if you know when to lean in. I kiss her on her cheek, swiftly making a move down her neck. She closes her eyes in reflex and moans softly. She has on her favourite lime and black tank top. I gently move her hair to the front. The plunging neckline makes it easier for me to kiss the dragon tattoo on her right shoulder. And then, I get lost in her. I am transported to some other world, a world where everything is perfect. I regain my senses to realize that the coffee has turned cold. I completely lost track of time. She is lying next to me. My hands still holding hers, her legs around mine.

When you make love to someone, you bare your soul to them. You believe that the other person is not a different body, but a part of you, someone who understands you more than you understand yourself. I don't wish to hide anything from her.

I kiss her right hand, 'Darling! I have been working on a start-up idea for the past six months now.'

'You should stop hanging out with Sandy so much. He is a big loser, and wants you to join the club as well.'

'It is not about him,' I look into her eyes. 'It is about me.'

'Your father has left you enough wealth. Why would your uncle let you mess with the money?'

'I am not going to ask him for a single penny!'

'Baby, you've gone crazy!'

'Maybe, yes. I have gone crazy!'

She dresses up to leave for her yoga class, 'Give it another thought!'

A relationship can make you feel either fulfilled or hollow. I mostly feel hollow. Isn't love 'the everything' each one of us seeks in this world? There could be a lot of destinations, but isn't love the journey that we want to be part of?

I WhatsApp Sandy.

Kabir: She totally freaked out. I lost the bet.

Sandy: Bought two tickets for a start-up event. Leave office by 4 p.m. on Monday. Location: Cida de Palace.

Kabir: Dude! Hold a seat for me. Will see you there.

Morning messages can make or ruin your whole day. But messages like this really make my day! I reheat my coffee and stand on the balcony. The clock reads 7 a.m. The world looks beautiful in the early hours.

Only Sandy knows who it is I truly want to become.

THE ROUTINE

Myra

Monday, 12 December 2016
Cubicle 80
Mumbai, India

'City lights seem glorious at night, the high-rises stand in splendour, in my mind I have a fight, what do I want in life? I wonder!'

Madness! Stop, stop, stop, stop. 'I am waking up,' I scream as I bury my face in my pillow. I sigh, 'Tenth Snooze!' and turn the alarm off. It's funny how at night you don't feel like sleeping and in the morning you don't feel like waking up.

I sluggishly get up to do my morning 'rituals'. Monday begins, like any other day, on the toilet seat. I hear a noisy exhaust with snippets of farting at fixed intervals. My forty-year-old neighbour certainly has constipation, if not diabetes. I light a cigarette.

My small-towner granny had once said, 'The best way to start your day is to take a brisk walk in the park.' This was when I had visited her years back. Back then I had said we were too busy for that bullshit in the city. Now, I wish I could see her one last time.

I move my fingers on Buddy's skin. I begin with *On the Open Road*. I think of Ramy before I go to sleep, I think of him after I wake up! Sometimes, I feel like he is not someone else, but a part of me which has been missing for a long time. No update. I presume he must be camping in the wilderness of Savannah or floating in the Dead Sea.

I right swipe on Buddy to dump all notifications into the trash. WhatsApp messages. Facebook notifications. Instagram posts. Cute dogs and cats, some friends posting pictures from exotic places, some graduating, some switching jobs and some getting married. Does someone feel like breaking up? I do. I am going to put 'that' as my status soon. A Facebook profile reflects a happier version of you from an alternative reality, but your happiness is as up for contention as the theory of parallel universes.

The top five emails in my brutally honest account are highly predictable. They just appear in a newer order:

Myra, exciting job openings await you in your area for tele callers, click to find more.

Should you skip the $69 flight to the US?

Crush the December rush. Hurry now. Grab the sweet deal!

Congratulations! Click here to claim your iPhone 7 now!

Wanderlusting, are you? Escape now on a shoestring budget to Europe's best destinations!

'A software developer's profile can't be misunderstood for a tele caller! I might be a desperate job seeker but I am certainly not a beggar.'

My reverie breaks and I reach to flush the toilet. I don't dare to do otherwise! I belong to the pack, the commuters of the local train. We are prisoners of the clock and satisfy our souls by dancing to the music that goes tick-tock, tick-tock.

I turn up the radio. Mornings with Vicky airs exactly when I dress up for another day at India's largest IT factory.

'We are all here for a purpose,' booms RJ Vicky.

I hopelessly stare into the mirror in front of me, 'Am I?' You can lie to the world on social media but this is one of those rare moments when reality slaps you hard in the face.

Rhea enters the room.

'It is good to see that you're up on time,' she smiles as she watches me get ready for yet another day at the cubicle where I have spent countless weeks.

'Two years and counting, still a routine seems as difficult to attain as the Everest!'

She touches the radio, 'Soon it will be passé like the telegram. Saavn and Gaana are trending now like Instagram!'

I defend the radio. 'I love it.' It reminds me of Ramy. It is crazy how you bond over weird stuff with your childhood friends. It can be orange candies, the smell of the first rain, the sight of a sand castle on the beach or an old bicycle.

'Will you have cornflakes?' Rhea asks.

'Yes!' We move to the small dining table adjacent to our kitchen. When we are not running late, occasionally, we treat ourselves to cornflakes soaked in cold milk.

She places two bowls on the table, 'It is the easiest stuff to prepare.'

I adjust my girth to button the trousers. I have lost my appetite but I put on weight steadily due to a ridiculous eat-work-roam-sleep pattern.

We run to the station. The crowd doubles with every passing minute!

Same time. Same station. Same train. Same faces.

'What are you going to tell Neerav?'

'Yes!'

She freaks out, 'Have you informed your family?'

'I don't owe anyone an explanation,' I retort.

We board trains headed in opposite directions. I travel towards the south.

The electro-mechanical wheels of the train move us. I wish we were moved by desire, thought or passion. I reluctantly stand among people with derailed dreams. I fiddle with Buddy, and so does my pack. To break the monotony of life, we watch videos, listen to music and play games. Some talk to themselves mindlessly—that's the worst nightmare you can witness coming to life!

Without much effort, I am herded to get down at the Vikhroli station.

The IT factory is a huge glass building, the kind that excites university students enough to study their arses off and undergo metamorphosis that turns them into employees. Employees connect by the disgust they share—for the boss and the company, in that order—but are physically divided by the cubicles that stretch on till the end of sight.

Arun is a supercilious jerk who makes offensive remarks now and then. He attracts universal hate. When he targets me, I retaliate with the weapon called 'smile' from my arsenal. He observes all of us like a hawk. He knows exactly what his subordinates are up to at any point in time. For instance, he knows the exact time Samar spends in the loo when he is not in his seat. He makes sure he gives me a wicked smile whenever I accidentally glance at him. I make sure I innocuously smile back.

He smiles at me. I do not smile back.

Arun complains as usual, 'You're late again!' 'It will not happen again,' I assure him.

Neerav is grinning widely. I smile back. We are the partners-in-crime on the third floor. Neerav occupies the cubicle next to mine. He is the guy with relevant work experience, who can fix any bug in the software code for anyone. At times, colleagues call him Neeravji out of sheer love and reverence.

Kanika occupies the cubicle to my left. She prefers mincing words than arguing with anyone. When she does not reply, it is her way of rebellion.

Samar, a geek who has a crush on me, occupies the one in front. He eavesdrops on every conversation happening around.

'Why didn't you turn up last night?' I complain. 'Where?'

'At Starbucks 24x7! You missed an opportunity to meet Kashyap. He can guide us with our start-up in the future.'

'Did you call me? Or text me?'

'Call!'

'I don't remember. I slept early yesterday.'

Samar raises an eyebrow. Like every other occasion, we choose to ignore him completely.

Neerav points to his watch and suggests to wait until lunchtime.

'Did you go through the news?' Neerav quizzes at the lunch table.

'No,' I confess.

He seems annoyed. He says after a pause, 'As usual! I always ask you to stay updated.'

I make an attempt to pacify him, 'Ok, Tell me! What's wrong?'

'Nothing is wrong. Every time I turn on the social media updates or read newspapers, I feel the fear of missing out. There are guys out there, already pursuing their ideas. On top of that, some have even got investors on board to back their ideas. Unlike us, who just talk!' He leans over and picks up a business newspaper from the next table. He straightens it out and carefully places it on the table. 'Here, have a look,' he says, his eyes dancing in excitement.

'Aerospace start-up raises $20 million to fully fund a moon trip,' I read out loud.

'A trip to the moon! The Westerners have gone crazy.' I feel startled. He smiles and says, 'But our country will soon follow in their footsteps. These start-ups are suddenly valued at billions, if I put all the worth together! This is the time to be in the start-up space,' he says.

I overhear the conversations happening in the background. A guy is going crazy mocking the HR. Some are bitching about their bosses. Some are discussing their farfetched dreams of pursuing ideas just like mine.

In the second half, Arun comes around and announces, 'Your income will get doubled!' It is loud enough to grab eyeballs from every cubicle. Some are left with their tongues hanging out. This is not a strange reaction though. When you work in the IT sector, getting a salary hike is as exhausting as getting a woman to orgasm. It takes quite an effort.

'Have you suggested my name to the HR for an appraisal?' This is the longest I speak with him, by any measure, time or words. At least an orgasm leaves you moaning.

Arun turns towards me and says, 'Your US visit is approved. Get in touch with the travel desk!'

My blood freezes. I become confused about how to react. I don't know what to do with this piece of news. After a two-minute pause, I say, 'Yes, I will.'

Neerav frowns. He looks into my eyes and whispers, 'I will have to look for another co-founder. Why were you so actively involved in the discussions if you had no serious intention? It's hard to understand what your true priority in life is!' He picks up his stuff in a huff and leaves.

Rhea comes running to my room that night and hugs me. 'Congratulations,' she says.

'How do you know?' I hold her back.

'Samar posted a congratulatory note on your wall. Everyone knows,' she mutters.

Fuck.

A notification pops up on *On the Open Road*. It reads, 'We belong to a generation full of broken hearts and wandering souls, just blank from the inside, in constant search of ourselves, looking for something we don't know yet, in the empty spaces of life. It is not that we can't do great things, but we're raised to believe we can't!'

I WhatsApp Neerav.

Myra: Hey! I am not sure if I did the right thing! I am sorry to have let you down. Can we talk about it again?

Blue ticks appear, which bring a smile to my face. I keep waiting but he does not reply. Three hours now. No reply yet. Maybe, I should walk up to him tomorrow.

. I note down, 'City lights seem glorious at night, the high-rises stand in splendour, in my mind I have a fight, what do I want in life? I wonder!'

BACK-SEAT WISDOM

Kabir

Monday, 12 December 2016
Seat 80
New Delhi, India

'As a young graduate, I was full of fear, be it
about the future or failure, and that led to all
the wrong decisions in my career.'

On the days when I am working on a project that is too close to my heart, I feel like a social worker who rescues underprivileged kids. On other days, I feel like I am the one who needs to be rescued. I feel like a social worker after attending the kind of events I am going to today.

If I am not talking to Buzo, I am mostly talking to Siri.

'Siri, how far is Cida de Palace from my office?'

'Cida de Palace is 17 kilometres from your office as the crow flies.'

'Siri, remind me to leave office at 4 p.m.'

'Sure thing, Kabir.'

After office, I drive to Cida de Palace in my Audi R8. I don't care about the traffic, the distance, or the highway. I just love to drive. The screen on the front mirror powered by Google helps me navigate. I have made every single effort to make my car's interiors look like the ones from sci-fi movies.

My uncle once suggested that one should be driven around by a chauffeur. It saves one enough time to strategize future moves in the back of the car! After all, time is money. I replied, 'I do everything as you say but I am not going to hire a chauffeur.' This thought makes me drive like an untameable rebel, changing lanes quickly, accelerating and braking hard to screeching tyres. I reach there ten minutes before the estimated time. I make sure to grab an Americano on the way.

As I step into the auditorium, I see at least a hundred aspiring entrepreneurs gathered there to absorb the wisdom. The question which intrigues me is: How many of us will actually take it up? I can't vouch for any other, as I can't even take my own responsibility. My uncle is not the only villain in the world.

Everyone has taken their place by now. I call Sandy to check where the fuck he is? I don't like when people are late. If there is a thing I have learnt from my business trips abroad, it is respecting and valuing others' time as much as your own. He disconnects my call, but the very next moment, I see him flashing his phone from a distance. Oh, God! He has taken one of the rear seats again!

'You could not locate a place any further?' I say as I walk over to him.

'Looks like you're used to the VIP seats and the business class now!'

'No, it is not about the comfort, it is about the distance.

What is the logic of choosing a back seat all the time?'

He elaborates in the most animated way, 'The convenient seat function f is dependent on two parameters x and y, where x means the farthest seat attainable from where the speaker stands and y means minimum humiliation faced while figuring the seat out.'

Then he continues with a grin, 'The search ends when you reach the farthest seat beyond which no more humiliation can be faced!'

'You're talking like a psycho engineer now!'

Then I scan him from top to bottom. He is wearing green chinos and a printed shirt. 'What's up with your clothes? I thought these were only meant for those boys-on-the-beach print ads.'

'Dude, look around, you are the only one who has suited up. What are you here for? Donating half a million dollars in the name of CSR?'

'I have come directly from office!'

'Do you remember the last time you felt free enough to put on what you wanted to?'

'Okay. Stop it. You've all the gyan, buddy.'

'I have a question, though.'

'What?'

'Do you ever take this Apple watch off your wrist?'

'No.'

'I knew it. I knew that you fuck naked with that piece of technology around your wrist,' he laughs at me.

'Technology has always excited me. As a child, I preferred to dissect the toy car than to drive it!' I defend my obsession with gadgets.

I look up just then and get a glimpse of the emcee who is on the stage, looking after some arrangement along with the backstage team. She is drop-dead gorgeous with a perfect bosom and butt.

'She is the kind each one of us wants to fuck,' Sandy says.

'Buddies think alike,' I agree with him. It's funny how men can never argue differently over hot women.

I often wonder what it feels like to be in love? Even Karen, the most gorgeous girl at the university, fails to make me hold back my desires! While I am lost in my own world, sipping on the Americano, the gorgeous woman takes the spotlight.

She introduces herself as Jennifer and takes us through the schedule, creating a sense of curiosity around the speakers. She mentions a surprise address by the Asia-Pacific business head of a major international energy giant.

As the hours pass, entrepreneurs come up on the stage and talk about their struggles and journeys. Some emphasize the benefits of failure, while some talk about grabbing the opportunities that come your way. All I understand is: Every journey is unique and while their stories are good enough to inspire me, I will have to write my own unique story.

Finally, it is time for the surprise address.

The spotlight accompanies the addresser as he walks towards the podium. There are whispers across the hall as most people recognize him. He is none other than Rajat Kapur, the off-beat Hindi film actor. He has done quite a few regional theatre shows as well. But what none of us knew about him is that he also heads such a great business!

The moment he starts to speak, I realize he is one of those speakers who are perfect storytellers and keep their audience engaged with an extremely engrossing speech. I take down notes as I aspire to address the employees of my company in the best possible way. There is something so good about being grounded and able to connect with people.

'It is quite easy to take an impulsive decision when you are young. The ability to take risks and follow your heart tapers off as you grow old. This might not be a fact, but I have experienced it in my encounters with people from all walks of life. I have been an observer since childhood and love understanding and studying people,' he says.

He giggles as he continues, 'Now you see, that is the problem. I never went on to pursue a career in psychology!'

There is a long pause. Silence fills the huge room. I hear a crackling sound from the air-conditioning vault right above my head. Then, I notice that he is shivering as he sips his coffee. It spills from the spotless white ceramic cup on to his Armani blazer. The other sound is of the cup clinking on the saucer. He grabs a tissue paper and cleans the mess.

All eyes are on him.

'As a young graduate, I was full of fear, be it about the future or failure, and that led to all the wrong decisions I made in my career,' he carries on.

'After forty-five, I decided to pursue theatre and drama because I loved it, and had enough money to sustain myself if things didn't work out.'

He suddenly throws a question our way, 'Do you think I am successful?' As he breaks the monotony, he succeeds in gaining the attention of even the fellow sitting at the farthest end, which is our row. People who are busy on their phones or are having a short nap, become alert. He proves that the earlier pause was just like a lull before the storm. I am convinced there is something more to it, something graver coming our way. This guy is behaving like a musician tripping on a narcotic substance.

On the contrary, he resumes in a distinctively low voice. 'I am unsuccessful. I don't want you to follow me. All I want to tell you is, do what you love. I was money-driven. I just succeeded in filling up my bank account in the first forty-five years of my life,' he confesses. His hands shiver violently each time he lifts the cup, only to clumsily place it back on the saucer. His voice loses volume at the end of each statement, which prompts me to tip my hat to the inventor of the collar mic.

'The two things that make me to go to bed peacefully at this age are my rehearsals at the drama institute and Angelina,' he adds. The statement brings a sly smile to Sandy's face, who is sitting next to me. He looks at me with a meaningful expression which essentially tells me that whatever Rajat is saying is true and I might end up like him some day.

'Angelina is my two-year-old cat. She is neither my wife nor my daughter, and definitely not my girlfriend,' he adds. 'If you think it is easy for me to say this, since I already have money, I would like to add that it would have been much more satisfying if I had earned it through theatre.' He is clearly regretful.

A guy from the back row yells, 'What a poor fellow!' and looks around to exchange looks with others. Nobody reciprocates. It is one of those moments when most of us empathize with his pain. We are scared to the core about ending up on stage like him someday.

He concludes, 'Always remember, the real struggle in life is not doing what you love, it is not even making money. The real struggle in life is to make money doing what you love.'

It takes balls to be so honest on a professional podium. I stand to cheer him for being so honest. I can't help clapping. Sandy looks at me with a sly grin and joins me. Others soon follow and the hall echoes with a thundering applause.

Rajat smiles back at all of us and leaves clumsily. He stumbles as he approaches the corner of the stage and is finally escorted out by three men.

Sandy turns towards me and says, 'What do you think he was tripping on?'

'Something more fatal than grass. Chemical, I presume.'

'Yeah, I agree!'

As we make our way towards the parking, Sandy flashes his phone in my direction and says, 'Have a look at this.'

'What's it?'

'Read it.'

A notification from *On the Open Road* catches my attention. It has a quote that reads:

'We belong to a generation full of broken hearts and wandering souls, just empty on the inside, in a constant search for ourselves, looking for something we ourselves don't know yet, in the desolate spaces of life. It is not that we can't do great things, but we're raised to believe we can't!

'I want to meet Ramy.'

'Me too.'

I think of Rajat while driving back home. The loud claps that echoed in the magnificent hall iterate in my mind. I have thoughts of leaving everything behind and rebuilding my life from scratch. I have told myself a million times that I am going to leave, but it has never happened. I somehow end up on the same road that leads to my office.

Ramy says that some things are to be left to God, or serendipity, or the universe, that there is a bigger plan that we are all part of! I don't know if any of it is true for me.

What am I going to do next? The question haunts me. But where do I go? Finally, the digital slave in me finds a way out. Siri comes to my rescue.

'Where do I go, Siri?'

'I don't have an opinion on that.'

'I want to leave everything.'

'I am not sure I understand.'

'What if I die?'

'I am afraid I don't know the answer to that, Kabir.'

I lie in bed anxiously. I pat Buzo and make him sleep next to me. He makes me feel loved with an incomparable sense of security. I turn on the TV but keep glancing out of the window and back to the TV in a strange pattern. I can't run away from my responsibilities. It will not be in the best interest of the people and the company.

WAKE UP CALL—I

Myra

Friday, 16 December 2016
Nirvana Biker's Cafe
Mumbai, India

'Once you have fallen into the EMI trap, not
much can be done!'

Life goes on, exactly the way I work in my cubicle. Copy. Paste. Copy. Paste. Copy. Paste. Except, I feel lost. More lost than ever. Neerav has disappeared into thin air. Neither Arun nor my colleagues know of his whereabouts. He does not return my calls either.

'Neerav is such a crucial resource. Without him, everything in the department seems to be paralyzed,' Arun grimaces as he passes a file to Kanika. The uneasiness I have been experiencing makes me react audaciously, 'In the pool of a thousand employees who work on the same shit every day, is anyone really crucial?'

Arun's disgust knows no bounds. He leaves for his cabin, raging with anger. While they are the ones who bitch about Arun in the cafeteria every day, I become the outlet of their true feelings in this very moment.

Nobody supports me. My colleagues pretend to be busy writing code on their laptops. In the IT factory, you have colleagues, not friends.

'You're screwed,' Samar mocks.

'Shut up, stalker! Mind your shit!' I yell at him.

My colleagues look at me with sympathy. They certainly think I have gone crazy. I know they are a bunch of slaves. Fair enough!

I open the WhatsApp chat window a zillionth time and message Neerav.

Myra: Hi! I know you are mad at me. Plz get back asap as I am starting to worry.

No blue ticks. It disappoints me. I check Buddy for a blue tick now and then. Work? I can't focus on anything. I play games on Facebook instead.

On the way back home, Buddy starts to buzz, the vibrations synonymous with WhatsApp messages. I pull it out of the laptop bag in excitement. I touch the screen. My excitement comes to a standstill as I see Rhea's messages instead.

Rhea: Saurabh and I are headed to the college reunion party. Gimme a call once you are free!

I don't reply. On reaching home, I pour myself a glass of wine. I dim the lights in my room and play some light music, jazz to be precise, to relax myself. As hours slide, I am lulled into a peaceful sleep.

Buddy buzzes yet again. I reach for it with much difficulty. I find it somewhere amidst my pillows and the sheet. I fail to identify the number, but answer anyway.

'Hello, Myra!' Arun greets me. He never calls so late at night. I am both nervous and excited. After all, this call could be regarding my brazenness at the IT factory.

'Hello!'

'I have got some news,' he says in a grave tone.

When people tell you that they have got news, the chances of it being good or bad are equal. Deep down, however, you know you are far more willing to deal with the good one.

Then, there's a long pause. I feel uncomfortable. 'Good news?' I quiz in excitement.

'Bad,' he confirms.

My heart throbs faster. My heartbeat sound like gunshots being fired in the air.

'Samar is a better fit for the on-site assignment, therefore I have approved his visit in consultation with the US office.'

'What? But my credentials and profile exactly fit the requirements. I can't miss this opportunity!' I mutter endlessly in an attempt to pacify myself with a false belief that my unintelligible blabber, a manifestation of my hopelessness, affects him.

'One should not mess with the boss,' he interrupts in an assertive tone to put a full stop to my rant. I now know he is a true monster and nothing can melt him.

'Two pieces of bad news. This day must be difficult for you.'

I cross my fingers. I silently pray that the other news is not as bad as the first one, 'What's the other news?'

'It seems you're totally unaware!' 'Of what?' I say bluntly.

'Unfortunately, our beloved Neerav passed away. His car was retrieved from the valley along the Mumbai–Pune expressway,' he says in a cold voice.

It feels like life has been sucked out of me.

'I hate you. I hate bosses. I hate myself. I hate this life!' I scream hard, without realizing the implications it may have in future. Arun hangs up. The news terrifies me inside out. I feel devastated. I want to talk to someone, someone who understands me, someone I can share the sorrow with, a shoulder to cry on. I call Sid, over and over.

Sid calling. Sid calling. Sid calling . . .

Time stands still. I don't give up. I stare at the screen and keep calling. Aren't twenty-five missed calls enough for him to call me back? I feel a huge stone-like lump in my throat that can neither be swallowed nor be thrown up. It erupts at the back of my throat; the waves travel to my chest causing inexplicable pain. I break down eventually, in endless tears. Arun's words reverberate in my mind, again and again, till it dizzies me.

I work myself into a frenzy and turn on the lights, fans, every switch in the bedroom. I rush to the wall and look at the sticky notes in disdain. I start pulling them out, one by one, starting with the orange note, and tear them apart to the last bit. I run. I scream. I wail. I search for my prescription pills in the bedside drawer and find them missing. Rhea keeps moving things all the time. I hate her for this. I don't rest until I have lit up the entire apartment. I feel as if I need to get away from the darkness as soon as possible and move towards the light.

I look out of the window at the view of the madness that is Mumbai. I imagine the intensity of his desire to quit this job and start up a company with me. He was about to take a step forward, but everything came to an end for him. I have never felt emptier before. I gulp a few more glasses of wine to run away from the thoughts that cloud my mind.

I book a ride on Ola and leave home wearing just my slippers, pyjamas and a loose black t-shirt; a blue sling bag and Buddy accompany me. In an attempt to lock the main door, keys slip out of my hands and slide down the staircase. 'Fuck,' I scream as I make an attempt to pick them, but kick them further down instead.

Shantaram stares at me, eyes wide open. I choose to ignore him.

I get into the cab and put my head against the backrest to get temporary relief from the dizziness. The driver accelerates uniformly. I recite a few lines of the song 'Let It Be' over and over, 'When I find myself in times of trouble, mother Mary comes to me, speaking words of wisdom, let it be, let it be, let it be, let it be, let it be, let it be, let it be, let it be!'

Someone interrupts in a feeble tone, 'What's your destination?'

I notice an old man sitting next to me. His face looks pale but as calm as the moon; his eyes are wrinkled around the corners, and a mix of blonde and grey locks stretch down to his chin and seamlessly mingle with his long beard. I presume he is a traveller from the West.

I unlock Buddy to discover that I have booked an Ola Share in haste. I hear my mother's grim disapproval at the back of my head—it is not safe for girls to move around alone in the city so late. I hardly give it a second thought and decide to go ahead.

'What's your destination, lady?' he stresses. 'Nowhere,' I turn towards the old man, 'I want to go nowhere,' I stutter as I look into his eyes.

'Your destination shows Wayfarer Street,' the driver interrupts. 'What place is that?' I inquire and then burst into laughter. I must have touched any random place on the map as the destination. 'Keep driving,' I instruct the driver.

'What's your destination?' I ask the old man in curiosity. 'Wayfarer Street,' he smiles back. Same pickup, same drop! That's a bizarre coincidence! The driver gives me a blank look as our eyes meet in the rear-view mirror. Nonetheless, he follows my command.

'Take control of your life and head in the direction you want to. Your mind will be at peace when you do something that your heart wants! Days will turn into months and months into years. Getting sloshed is not a solution,' the old man whispers into my ear.

'What?' I ask curtly.

The driver interrupts, 'Do you need help?'

'Mind your own business!'

I turn towards the old man and say, 'Today is the lowest point of my life, I have hit rock-bottom. I don't need to hear anybody's advice.'

'You were about to fall into the EMI trap,' his tone changes from pleasing to concerned.

I respect the fact that he is older, yet warn him against overwhelming me with bits of advice, 'You make no sense, old man!'

'Peter,' he makes an attempt to calm me down.

'Peter, I suppose you're on a trip to India and all that fascinates you is the holy cow, the Ganga, Goa, Rishikesh and the Himalayan grass.'

'I am from Jordan,' he interrupts.

'Please leave me alone,' I snap back.

'Myra, dear, I am sorry for being nosy. This is what age does to you!' He gently smiles.

'How do you know my name?' My eyes are wide with equal surprise and disgust.

'I have access to the same ride,' he shows me the screen.

How dumb can I get? He is only trying to be nice. I feel guilty for being so rude. His sense of maturity and aura fascinate me. Suddenly, I feel an urge to talk to him. I ask hesitantly, 'Peter! What's the EMI trap?'

'Are you in the mood to listen? You will have to keep quiet for a while,' he says firmly but with a reassuring, patient look.

I instruct my mind to be receptive, 'Yes.'

'You earn money, spend some, and save the rest. Then, you start to earn more money, but save less as you tend to spend more. It progresses with the help of credit cards and EMIs. When you owe more than you have, you need a stable source of income to repay.'

'So?'

'Can you risk the security of your job?'

'No.'

'You have to pay for your credit card bills and EMIs.'

'Yes.'

'This is how you get stuck in the EMI trap,' he explains.

'But my situation isn't that bad. You make it sound worse!' I mutter.

'Here's the catch. You're young and free in a lot of ways that you would not be after ten years. Once you fall into the EMI trap, not much can be done,' he adds with an optimistic laughter.

I listen to him with childlike curiosity. I nod, looking straight into his eye. His conviction speaks volumes about the vastness of his experience.

The EMI trap. The EMI trap. The EMI trap.

The words keep swimming in my mind. I am stuck in a desert where no direction leads home; in search of my inner calling that seems to smile at me from a distance. It is like a mirage, seemingly deceitful, yet alluring. I want to walk up to it, but I can't find the way. All I can think about is Neerav's death.

'My friend . . . Neerav . . . he's no more. I let him down. And I want to go to the US, but my boss is now pissed at me. I wish there were a time machine for me to go back and fix all the things I have messed up,' I continue to complain, until he interrupts me in a firm voice, 'You must look ahead and embrace what the future holds for you.'

'Everything has gone for a toss,' I cry.

'You are not living your dream yet. You're living someone else's dream. The most tragic part is that you've forgotten the starting point of this process. It dates back to your birth,' Peter says to break the monotony of my tears. 'Everything, your name, your job, your life, has been chosen by someone else,' he adds.

'Madam, Madam, Madam, Madam!' the driver says in an attempt to wake me up. I squint my eyes and regain consciousness slowly. Frantically, I look to my side. There is no one there.

'Where is Peter?' 'Who?'

'The old man who was sitting here! Where is he?'

'Madam, there was no one else in the car,' he assures me. 'I am pretty sure he was there. We had the same destination. Did he get down before me?' I ask.

'You have been sleeping and mumbling all the way. I offered help but you asked me to keep driving.'

'Is this place safe to get down at?'

'Don't worry, madam! This is the street that never sleeps, the safest place in Mumbai.'

'Thank you for dropping me safely,' I smile at him, overwhelmed with gratitude. He truly deserves a five-star rating. My Paytm wallet takes care of the rest. I remember Kashyap, who always says, 'We can build a better India through entrepreneurship.'

'It's my duty, ma'am. Take care!' he smiles warmly.

I have not been to this place before. Wayfarer Street runs parallel to Henry Road on one side and Walton Road on the other. I saunter towards a familiar junction—the end of the street that meets the Colaba Causeway Market. Peter is all I can think of. After a series of nightmares, he is the best dream that has happened to me.

There is great rejoicing and festivity all around. The street is studded with cafes and shops on either side, lit up from one end to the other like an old bazaar from the Arabian Nights. The travellers are dressed like hippies from the late 1970s. The cosy compartments represent countries from all over the world. I look at each board: The Paris Cafe, The Baker Street Bookshop, Moroccan Delight, China Town, Burma Tea Cafe, The Himalayan Tree Adventures, Old Dubai Souk, Nirvana Biker's Cafe.

Nirvana is exactly what I want today! The board on the door reads,

Nirvana Biker's Cafe

11 Wayfarer Street,

Colaba,

Mumbai

As I push the door open, I hear the song 'Eye of the Tiger' playing in the background. The travel cafe has turned into a dim-lit rock club, walls tastefully done with photographs of bikers from around the world. It is predominantly occupied by travellers, mostly backpackers. The big bike wheel clock reads 12 a.m. My eyes search for a solitary corner to escape the crowd. I don't want to attract people's unwanted attention. I locate a long bench meant for accommodating multiple solo visitors, firmly placed against a giant glass wall through which the street is visible. Call it half-solitary, as the chatter from the adjacent tables is ineluctable.

I put my head on the table as it seems almost impossible to get over the thoughts of everything that has happened. Suddenly, a loud voice pierces the air, 'Wasn't Tawang a beauty?'

I turn to see Ramy making his way towards me with a beer mug in his hand. I am ecstatic, 'Yes, it absolutely was!'

'What the fuck are you doing here? I can't tell you how happy I am to see you.'

'Shut up!' He commands and escorts me to a rack nearby. He pulls out a bikers' road map, 'Today marks the completion of 30,389 miles,' and traces his index finger along the routes he has been on.

'Where the hell have you been for two long years?' I ask. I need answers.

'If something wonderful happens, you should drink to celebrate,' he says as he holds my right hand and drags me to the bar counter. I interrupt, 'What if something awful happens?'

He drags me close to him, looks into my eyes and says, 'Drink to forget.' He turns away and takes huge steps, his hand still holding mine.

'I am a few drinks down,' I admit.

'Two plus two beers,' he chimes to the bartender.

'You look awful in those chequered pyjamas. Looks like a guy's elongated boxers,' he laughs.

'I don't care!' I mumble.

'Do you sell meat to earn a living?'

'No.'

'Does someone from your family guard the Indo–Pak border?'

'No.'

'Then, cheer up.'

'I lost a colleague to a road accident!'

'So?'

'You've always been so insensitive,' I stress. 'Somebody close to me just died!'

'Isn't death the ultimate truth? You might die tomorrow. What lesson did you take back home from his death?'

'I don't want to die with any regrets.'

I know only he can save me tonight. I am thrilled to have him here, next to me. The song changes to 'Blowin' in the Wind' by Bob Dylan.

'Great. The last time we met you were quite dumb. I had to guide you. Life is the best teacher, I suppose,' he continues to sip beer from my glass, 'always remember, no one can steal your happiness, not even you! Your life is important.'

'These are claiming less lives than depression,' he says as he lights a cigarette, 'So why not just have a smoke and let things go with the wind for the moment?' I focus on the clouds of smoke with an amazing attention to detail. I follow the patterns which disappear into the air. Everything is so short-lived, just like the cigarette smoke. Maybe this pain will heal, sooner than the clouds of smoke dissolve. Like a rocket across the sky, this thought leaves a trail in my head. I don't fear death as much as the feelings that one's last thoughts leave right before it happens.

A white light seems to engulf the insides of my mind. It seems to tell me that if I can figure out a way to restart my life, I won't feel so dead inside. Maybe then the thought of death won't affect me as much, because I will live my life pursuing my dreams, like Neerav wanted it. It feels like this moment is what I have been waiting for all my life; a sense of awakening envelopes me. Only Ramy could do this to me.

In a way, although I have never visited the Wayfarer Street before, I belong here!

'Guess what my latest blog is about?'

'Me?'

'I don't want my fans to go away,' he laughs, 'It's about Nirvana Biker's Cafe.' He flashes the screen of his phone,

> *Nirvana Biker's Cafe is a hidden gem for backpackers in the lanes of Mumbai and Delhi.*
>
> *Somewhere between the 'right' and the 'wrong', the past and the future, there lies a 'now'. Don't let it go. For 'now' often leads to a new road! If you're still unsure about what you want to do, let yourselves loose on the open road. You will come back with an answer . . .*

He turns off the phone, 'Don't read any more!' He then takes me to the stage and screams, 'The girl in the awful pyjamas sings really well.'

'Sing out loud,' the crowd cheers.

'Sing out loud!'

'Sing out loud!' 'Sing out loud!' 'Sing out loud!' 'Sing out loud!'

I feel like a deserted rock star. The lights are dimmed and the spotlight finds me. I am a fearful one. I can't take centre stage. A huge panic attack engulfs me. I think I will collapse on the stage any moment.

Then, I see Ramy, clapping in the centre of the maddening crowd. The very next moment, my fear comes to a standstill. I read the lyrics of the song 'Hotel California' by The Eagles off a giant screen. I sing it on top of my voice, 'Her mind is Tiffany-twisted, she got the Mercedes-Benz. She got a lot of pretty, pretty boys, that she calls friends. How they dance in the courtyard, sweet summer sweat. Some dance to remember, some dance to forget!'

Ramy gets up on the stage, snatches the mic and suggests, 'We raise a toast to now; sing along with the songs in the background, like there is no tomorrow, no yesterday, only the moment in which we melt.'

The crowd goes berserk and follows his command.

'Find yourself!' he screams.

'Find yourself!' the crowd repeats.

'Love yourself!'

'Love yourself!'

I get down from the stage and go back to the solitary bench. I type 'bye bye losers' on WhatsApp.

I don't have the courage to hit the send button. Then, I un-type the entire message, character by character and re-type, 'bye-bye'. I delete it once again. I finally type, 'I don't wish to be found for some days' and send it to friends and family.

I type an email to my team to warn them against Arun's false promises and the massive fish trap that holds each one of us. I mark Arun in the cc as this will also serve as my resignation, the shortest in the history of the IT factory.

It reads, 'Once you have fallen in the EMI trap, not much can be done!'

I pull out the SIM card and place it, along with Buddy, in the inner pocket of the blue sling bag.

Ramy drags a chair next to me, 'Where are we headed next?'

'Himachal Pradesh!'

'Now you sound crazy. Just like me!'

'As long as you know who you are, I guess it is okay to be crazy,' I wink.

WAKE UP CALL—II

Kabir

Friday, 16 December 2016
Nirvana Biker's Cafe
New Delhi, India

'Somewhere between the "right" and the
"wrong", the past and the future, there lies a
"now". Don't let it go, for "now" often leads
to a new road!'

Sandy calls me at 6 a.m. It is unusual for him to call so early in the day.

'Hello!'

'Hi, Sandy!'

'Did you read the TechinIndia blog?'

'No. What's up?'

'The idea you elaborated the other day at the airport is taken!'

'What?'

'Yeah. They have raised a million dollars from a Japanese global investment firm.'

'Fuck!' I feel an instant shock encompassing my body.

I pack my backpack in unusual haste, constantly reaffirming that everything is going to be okay. When you own at least a hundred pairs of footwear, life looks complicated. But today, everything feels relatively simple. I pack only three pairs of clothing and no extra pair of shoes besides the ones on my feet. I assort the bottles of toiletries I have scooped from my exorbitant corporate visits.

Ramy tells us that the secret to life is to plan for not more than a week and try to live in the moment. Upper-class upbringing lands you in a state of confusion though. It demands you to maintain a status, yet stay frugal at heart!

'Stuff your backpack and get my Harley serviced.'

'Why?'

'We're leaving!'

'When? Where?'

'Let's decide that later tonight! I will come to see you.'

'Are you sure you want to do this?'

'I have never been surer of anything else!'

I call up my uncle's chauffeur to drive me to the office. I look at myself in the rear-view mirror of the car, reassuring myself that no matter what happens, I will be the sole decision maker of my life and do only what I want.

'Sir, you're doing the right thing!'

'What am I doing? Why would you say that?'

'You're just like your father. I have known him and the company for forty years now. Did your uncle never tell you how the idea of establishing this business popped up in his head?'

'No, never. Tell me,' I have never been more curious.

'Your dad went hitchhiking across Asia in the 1970s, from Istanbul to Hong Kong, covering all the trade hotspots on the way. I suppose you're also going on a long journey, really long,' he winks. There is a strange sense of conviction and calm in his eyes.

'Thanks for that bit of information, Ravi.' I wish I knew about this years ago. I would have left much earlier.

There is a sudden boost of energy and confidence in me. Knowing that my dad would undoubtedly have taken my side, rebelling against my uncle bothers me even less.

Bibek, the security guard employed at the main entrance of my office building, does not greet me. I walk past him, towards the elevator and press 'level three'. The button turns red. It looks like even the office elevator is warning me against entering it.

Everybody stares at me. Some are barely able to suppress their laughter, while the others look displeased. Nobody expects their CEO to wear a biker suit to office, or carry a big backpack.

I am not surprised as I look at myself in the elevator mirror. For the first time, I feel like I am looking at myself. The board members and company folks will assemble in the boardroom on the third floor at 10 a.m. sharp.

I glance at my Apple watch. It reads 09.47 a.m. 'Thirteen minutes to go,' I sigh as I settle into my seat, where I am at the helm of affairs. This black chair speaks of the huge responsibilities and the high stakes. Sometimes, your desire to follow your heart costs you more than just money. It costs you people's love and trust. Some things are harder to give up than others. Resigning as the CEO is not only a life-changing decision, but also a tough one.

Ramy tells us that sometimes it is worthwhile to look at the bigger picture and endure the pain some decisions cause. These should be made for long-term goals and not myopic ones. Some sacrifices are part of everyone's journey, especially the kind that is inward.

For the first time in my life, I am in the boardroom without any preparation. I don't know how I am going to address the investors and the fellows. I just have a piece of paper on which I have written some points. I set up the projector with the office boy. I instruct him to drag a whiteboard from the rightmost corner of the room.

I check and re-check my Apple watch. I haven't been this nervous in conscious memory.

9.55 a.m.

People begin to filter in and take their seats. My anxiety escalates proportionately to the passing of time. Everyone looks at me with a weird sense of rejection in the boardroom. Maybe it is my clothes, or my demeanour. They refrain from making sarcastic remarks though. The greyheads are a little too sophisticated to do that.

9.57 a.m.

One of the biggest challenges is to convince people elder to you. Their work experience makes them hardwired and unreceptive to new ideas.

9.58 a.m.

Maybe I should start with the benefits of embracing tech start-ups for their revolutionary products and their ability to disrupt markets.

9.59 a.m.

Maybe I should explain my idea to them, so they can get a peek into what I want to do. If they appreciate the idea, they might support me and not judge me the way they would otherwise.

45 seconds.

Some gurus from early morning TV shows suggest: A positive bend of mind or a positive thought process is all we need to create better outcomes. So, rather than saying that I am going to quit, let me tell them that I am going to start something new.

30 seconds.

Maybe an example will work? Why go into the 'why' and the 'how' of my unexpected move, when I can explain with the help of an example?

10 seconds.

Oh, fuck! What do I say?

My eyes scan the room from the rightmost corner, stop at Mr Mehta's name card and then wander to the others. I try not to fixate on my unusually dry throat.

After being in business for this long, you know that you can count on the people who have stayed with you for long. He was with my dad through the good and the bad. I know he is gold.

I decide to start as I look straight into Mr Mehta's eyes.

'Before we start, I want each one of you to take the writing pad and answer the following question.'

Everyone looks at me with a sudden surge of frenzy. They were not expecting this meeting to be so blunt and straightforward. It could even be read as absurd. Their faces are a reflection of the questions that are popping in their heads.

'Write ten things that give you immense happiness.'

They look startled as if they have been asked to jump off a plane from 36,000 ft. What comes to me as a surprise is that the people who play with ten-figure numbers can't write ten fucking things that give them happiness!

Ugly pause. Weird silence. Widespread frowns.

'Okay, let me make this task easier for you. You can write five such things down.'

'What's wrong with you, son?' Mr Mehta asks me. His brow is creased like a formation of sand dunes in a desert, but his eyes are looking straight into the mirage because he believes there is hope. I wish he knew that nothing he said can make me stop.

Regardless, I am happy that at least someone bothered to interrupt. Argument kills you slowly, but silence kills you all at once.

'This is the only thing I want you guys to do, maybe the last.'

'What do you mean by "the last"?'

'Why are dressed up in these clothes?'

'I am going to reveal everything, but I want each of you to write those five things. I am leaving the boardroom for ten minutes. I want you to take your time, think about it before putting it down on paper.'

As I move out, I can hear the people talk among themselves. They didn't even wait for me to fully exit. I overhear some whispering,

'This guy is rash.'

'I knew it was going to happen.'

'What is he wearing?'

'What does he think of himself?'

'Even though he is younger than us, we have to listen to him!'

'We don't have an option.'

I walk back into the room and read their papers out loud. I ask them, 'When was the last time any of you did any of these?'

My uncle interrupts, 'If you decide to leave, you cannot come back, and if you do, you get nothing.'

'I don't fear that as much as I fear losing you forever! You can have it all.'

I exit the boardroom. My phone starts to buzz. Karen calling. Karen calling. Karen calling . . .

I keep disconnecting her calls. After nearly ten calls, she gives up and messages me on WhatsApp. Who can come to my rescue now?

Karen: Darling! I need to see you.

Kabir: Why?

Karen: Your uncle called me up and informed me that you're resigning from the position of CEO, leaving for somewhere, blah, blah, blah . . .

Kabir: Hmm . . . it's true.

Karen: Looks like you've made up your mind but can you please meet me one last time?

I don't want to meet her. Why didn't she approve of it when I candidly spoke to her about it. Why did she leave suddenly then? I have been with her for two years now. It is a difficult decision to make. You always want to give one last chance to the people you love. You can't help it. I might never come back, and I want to taste her fruity pink lipstick one last time. Or maybe, things can work out. Maybe she wants to show her support now. I reluctantly give in to my emotions and message her.

Kabir: 4ish?

Karen: Where?

Kabir: I will book a table for us at your favourite cafe.

Karen: La Epicure? Ok!

Kabir: See you!

She is wearing a low-cut royal blue dress and a pearl necklace around her neck. The white pearls perfectly complement the blue of her dress. She has left her straight hair loose; her tresses rest on her left shoulder. I can see a pearl sparkling on her right earlobe. She looks as gorgeous as the first time I asked her out to the fresher's party. She was crowned Miss Freshers back then. There is something so delightful each time you see your girl, especially when she is looking so sexy.

'So, are you planning to leave?' She rushes towards me and hugs me. I hold her loosely, still unsure whether I should hold her tight or not. My heart tells me I should hold her tight, but my mind cautions me, telling me to avoid all the emotional tension that the situation can cause between us. She tries to kiss me, but I move her away politely. I don't want to give into the temptation.

At this point in time, my career is as important as anything else, or perhaps more important than anything else. It's not that I do not love her; I do love her. If I know what love means, it is because of all the feelings I have had for her. I don't want to go, but I don't want to stay either. She will not let me go and if I stay here for a minute more, I won't be able to go.

She walks up to me, but does not ask me to stay. She tells me how wrong I am and why I should not even try to start a company on my own. She tells me I should stay away from Ramy's ideas as she believes he is crazy—a sick extremist.

Finally, there is an update from *On the Open Road!* It reads:

> *Nirvana Biker's Cafe is a hidden gem for backpackers in the lanes of Mumbai and Delhi.*
>
> *Somewhere between the 'right' and the 'wrong', the past and the future, there lies a 'now'. Don't let it go, for 'now' often leads to a new road! If you're still unsure about what you want to do, let yourselves loose on the open road. You will come back with an answer . . .*

Karen insists, 'Okay, so I am asking you for the last time, either you have the company and me, or neither!'

'Neither,' I say and walk off.

I call Sandy, 'I am all set to leave!'

'Where do we meet?'

'Nirvana Biker's Cafe, Hauz Khas Village,' I say and hang up.

KNOCKING ON HEAVEN'S DOOR

Myra

Saturday, 31 December 2016
Shiva Cafe, Kasol
Himachal Pradesh, India

'We are born several times in a lifetime. Mostly
in darkness. Sometimes, we're lost for days
before we spot the light.'

Ramy and I escaped. It is almost as if we were on a quest to actually live the adventures we dreamt of through the National Geographic diaries that we all grew up watching. I suggested that we cover the entire stretch from the pristine foothills of Uttarakhand to the arid desert of Ladakh, like migratory birds. We inched towards Himachal Pradesh, taking in all of Rajasthan's beauty along the way.

I often asked him, 'Can we be together?' But he explained, 'Our relationship is like that of the sun and the moon.' I realize that while he illuminates my existence yet somehow we can never be together.

Two weeks ago, I woke up to Ramy's note:

I am on the way to Ladakh. I wish to spend my time there till the first monsoon shower.

Now, you'll start to worry. I know it comes naturally to you, but you need to learn to be on your own. I have taught you everything that you should know for travelling solo as a woman.

You're liberated the very day you stop being dependent on anyone but yourself.

Remember, the road to freedom is always long and challenging. That's why it is worth giving a try. It is with life as it is with the treks, you don't fail if you do not make it to the destination, you fail when you give up during the journey. So, you've already passed your first test.

Things to do:

First, you'll be responsible for the initiative 'The Redemption Trails' in the Himalayas. Take the followers on a challenging trek and post about the experience on my blog.

Second, never forget that the ultimate goal is to inspire the community to pursue their ideas, come what may.

Third, move on in your life, professionally and personally. Take up a temporary job. You'll go broke in another ten days. Also, dare to fall in love again. I can't hold your hand forever.

Travelling solo does not mean being alone, it means enjoying the company of the people you've never met before. Not talking to strangers is one of the strangest things. Every person you know was a stranger, and if we were never to die, would not most of us become strangers again?

Till we meet again,
Ramy

He never stays for long. He prefers to leave. Being alone gets scary at times though. I have been robbed of cash, have slipped off a narrow road, collapsed out of fear as ten wild dogs attacked me.

Days are scary but nights are worse. Nobody ever tells you the downside of following your heart. It sometimes alienates you from everyone else, and sometimes, from your own self too. Once you've lost relationships, you question the emptiness of your own soul. There's a blank space which stretches till infinity on either side of your existence. You walk a lonely path, from midnight to dawn, and there is no coming back. Somewhere in the middle of this suffering, you fall asleep, until a nightmare wakes you up again. As you place a shivering hand on your heart, you tell yourself that you will be okay.

We are born several times in a lifetime. Mostly in darkness. Sometimes, we're lost for days before we spot the light.

Yet, I don't wish to go back to Mumbai. The only road in life is the one which lies ahead. Today, I embark on my ninth trek in the Himalayas, to Kheerganga, a meadow in Parvati Valley in the district of Kullu, under Ramy's initiative, The Redemption Trails. We want to encourage our fellow travellers—whether they have

Stuti Changle

been long lost or newly born—to start their lives from scratch, no matter their age, and pursue their ideas.

I hand out printouts of The Redemption Roadmap created by Ramy and me to the band of trekker travellers. The simple truths of life are listed here, wisdom that no school in the world offers in its classrooms.

1. Break free from digital devices.
2. Talk to strangers. Know their story.
3. Be fearless.
4. Love yourself.
5. Keep moving forward. Never look back.
6. Make your own rules.
7. Embrace hardships and failure.
8. Stay fit. Your body is your greatest asset.
9. Dare to fall in love. Again.

A group of twenty-five has assembled at Shiva Cafe, Kasol, a hedonists' haven in Himachal, known for its virgin cannabis blossoms. Spotting Israelis in Kasol is like spotting Russians in Goa. These are the places where you might end up feeling like a foreigner in your own homeland.

To boost the energy and confidence of the group, I say, 'This is not just a trek. This is a life-changing experience. The next twenty-four hours will be some of the most memorable ones of your lives.'

'Woohoo,' they cheer in unison.

I go over the itinerary, 'We will take a Himachal Tourism bus from Kasol to Barshaini village. From Barshaini, we will go to the Kheerganga peak via Rudra Nag, which is the midway stop.'

I see faces beaming with enthusiasm and optimism all around. Excited to set this party rolling, I ask, 'Any questions?'

'What is the difficulty level of the trek?' a young girl in red pyjamas quips.

'The round trip is around 28 km. This is not a very tough trek. We don't wish to be the next big mountaineers. The idea is to simply challenge and push ourselves to be able to do our best.'

'Let's start, folks!' shouts an overenthusiastic guy.

The trail is full of treacherous paths, but it has its perks.

The sunlight bounces off the mica pebbles strewn across the valley, creating intricate patterns. Parvati River can be heard roaring below, cutting across the mighty mountains looming over us. The path becomes perilously narrow at times, making you hope this isn't the last time you are peeping down at the meandering river.

'You are not Israeli, are you?' a guy from the group asks. He has been interested in talking to me since yesterday. I can sense the urge in his eyes. He has been following me, all the way up.

'What do I look like?'

'A young Indian girl in her mid-twenties, or maybe early. Your attire is causing some confusion though. You dress up like most of the Israeli men, especially in Kasol. Long cotton kurta, bandana, Afghani salwar, braided hair and the bold black kohl lining your eyes.'

'Keen observation, I must say.' We share a laugh.

'You're from Delhi, right?'

'Yes, I am. How did you deduce that?'

'Most Indians can spot Delhiites. It's our secret skill.'

'Now will you please tell me? Where are you from?'

'Nowhere.'

'Which city were you in before you came here?'

'Mumbai.'

'Fuck! Are you not going to talk to me any more, Ms Mumbaikar?'

'Yes, of course. Why wouldn't I? But isn't talking too much of a Delhi-thing?'

'I knew this was coming!'

'Myra,' I say as I extend my hand.

'Kabir,' he introduces himself.

'Where is your friend?'

'How do you know I am here with a friend?'

'I saw you guys checking me out last night at Shiva Cafe.'

'Oh! I am sorry. We were pretty high. We were trying to figure out what made you take the tough road!' he marvels.

He turns to look back. 'Sandy is walking at a slow pace. He is clicking breathtaking shots of the Himalayas on the way, I presume.'

Kabir continues to match my pace as the trail ascends. He offers a helping hand every time I am about to lose my balance, either on a loose boulder or the fragile accident-prone bridges. We come across frozen waterfalls, since winter is at its peak.

I point to a board on the way for the group members to see. It reads:

Amihay Cohen (R.I.P) (1975–1999)
Here fell and died a dear man and a good friend.
Young, full of joy, at the prime of his life.
Who was not careful enough taking this road. Please
do not take shortcuts.
Love you and always will.

I start, 'Do realize that if you have made it till this point in your lives, you're definitely here for a bigger purpose. Do what you wish to do before death takes it all away.' A tear rolls down my cheek as I think about Neerav. I wipe it off with the help of my scarf.

We make a halt at the checkpost near the Rudra Nag waterfall. Kabir makes an announcement amid the group savouring Maggi and tea, 'Move fast guys. This is just a fifteen-minute break. We need to make it to the top before the sunset.'

Sandy adds, 'Also, heavy rainfall is predicted for tomorrow. I suggest we start as early as possible, since we don't want to take chances with the river and landslides.'

'Thank you,' I smile back at them.

'What for?' Kabir seems puzzled.

'For volunteering!'

'The pleasure is all mine,' Sandy says.

'Myra,' I extend my hand.

'Sandeepan. You can call me Sandy, like most of my friends do!' he says, shaking my hand.

We finally arrive at the top at 5 p.m. Exhausted from the gruelling trek, everybody throws off their bags on the campsite. Panting still, heart racing from the 14-km-long ascent, I ask the group, 'How is the view?'

'It is magical.' 'Superb.' 'Extraordinary.' 'Beyond words.' I hear overlapping voices indicative of awe and ecstasy.

'You need to walk past the hardships when you take the road less travelled, to reach places where most people cannot.'

Kabir points to the peak adjacent to the meadow, 'These sulphur springs have magical healing powers. Soak yourselves and get rid of all the fatigue that this trek might have caused.'

'Also, nature has a cure for everything.' He says and winks at me.

While some savour energy drinks, some bandage their feet, some play their boomboxes, some soak in the hot water springs, and some lay on their back on the grass.

I look for a secluded corner to marvel at the evening sky. I gaze at the horizon. An enchanting sunset is underway. I catch myself skipping a few breaths as the vista unravels before my eyes. The crimson mountains are bathed in hues of red and gold, mirroring the sky.

Kabir walks beside me. 'We push ourselves hard to upgrade our lifestyle, which mostly means upgrading the clothes we wear, the perfumes we buy, the cars and bungalows we own. Yet, it is funny how we feel complete only when we lie bare on the soil.'

'True.'

He sits next to me, 'What brings you here?'

'A friend's death. A broken heart. An unsatisfactory job. A far-fetched dream of starting up a company. A lot of things, I must confess.'

'I am sorry about your friend. I could sense the pain in your voice when you pointed that board out.'

'What are you sorry about? Isn't death the ultimate truth?' I quip brusquely.

'I lost my parents in a car crash when I was five years old. Who knows the pain of losing someone more than me?'

'Now, I am sorry about that.'

He lights up a joint and skilfully changes the course of the discussion, 'Let's talk about better shit. Apart from some soul-searching, Sandy and I are here to work on a start-up idea.'

'That sounds interesting. What's the idea though?'

'We're still thinking about it. You usually don't have a single idea. You have a lot of them. The Herculean task is to figure out the best one.'

'How do you know which is the best one?'

'An idea that is not only conceivable, but also feasible.'

'I see.'

'So, we go to Rishikesh next, stay there for a week, finalize the idea and go back to the city.'

'Great! I hope to see you in the newspapers then, Mr Entrepreneur.'

'I don't know if we will make it to the Himachal Pradesh news headlines.'

He offers me the joint. I take a long drag in, out, in, out, three times, and hand the joint back to where it belongs. He takes a drag in, out, in, out, in, for . . . I lose count. Maybe three. Or two? Who cares?

'How long has it been since you hit the open road?'

'Two weeks roughly. We are big fans of *On the Open Road* and take the trips suggested by Ramy.'

'Oh! I am a fan too.'

'Have you met him?'

'No. I am doing this on a contract basis. He calls at times, but from a different number every time,' I say with a laugh. I can't tell the truth as Ramy does not want to meet anyone.

'Mysterious guy, a true modern nomadic yogi.'

He passes the joint to me. Yet again. Three drags, in and out, and I hand it back.

'You're a brave young woman,' he says candidly. After a long time, I feel good about myself. Surprisingly, he labels me 'brave', and not 'beautiful' or 'hot.'

'Thank you!'

He puffs the smoke out. This time, I don't know the count, but the smoke forms weird and unprecedented patterns, a dance more artistic than the ballet, a song sans music, a painting with unfathomable depth, and then it mingles with the surroundings and gets lost in the lap of the hills.

I decide to lie down and so does Kabir. Stars become visible, one at a time, then disappear in an endless interplay between light and infinity. Stars. Endless. Uncountable. Infinite. The constellations, the Pole Star, the small ones, the shooting stars. In my head, which is growing increasingly light, a plane skiing across the sky looks like a shooting star. After some time, the Milky Way becomes visible, as grandiose as it appears in the National Geographic photographs.

A joint triggers meaningful conversations, the kind you never knew you were capable of. The endless meadow of Kheerganga is a perfect setting for opening the doors to vivid imagination.

'I could not see the stars from my lavish balcony,' he breaks the silence.

'Me neither.'

He lifts his hand in awe and points ahead. 'Is that the Milky Way?'

'Yes, it is.'

'I am witnessing it with naked eyes for the first time.'

'I can relate to the feeling. A few days back, it was my first time. Post that, I stargaze every night.'

'What do you take back from all the stargazing?'

'A realization of how significantly insignificant we are!' 'The locals told me that according to a folklore, Lord Shiva meditated right here for 3000 years!'

'I wonder if it was that one infinite moment for him too.'

I turn towards him and say, 'They say that when people die, they become stars.'

'Science suggests that we are made up of star matter. Going by that, we were always stars, continue to be and will always be. But some stars like you lose their shine until some stars like me bring it back.'

Only a few people you will ever meet in your entire life will be able to hold your gaze and look into your soul. He knows that the sorrow of an ailing past connects us.

'I believe Neerav is right there in the night sky.'

He touches my head with his index finger playfully. 'No, Neerav is right there, and will always be. Memories stay forever, I believe, life and death can't do us apart.'

'That's an impressive thought, Kabir,' I say as I turn towards the sky again.

'I don't wish to know the details though.'

'Of Neerav and me?'

'Yeah. I hope he was not the guy you loved . . . '

I stay silent. After a while he asks me, 'Was he your boyfriend?' There is a hesitation in his voice and a deep urge to hear a 'No' in return.

'No.'

His face lights up with a faint smile. 'So, who was he?'

'He was the guy I was supposed to start a company with!'

He leans in. 'You can still start a company and show him some respect. It is never too late.'

I lean in, as if by reflex. The moment I feel I have got too close, close enough to feel his breath on my cheek, I back off. I have known him only for a couple of hours, yet I get the feeling of returning home after months. However, this feeling, as intense as it is, scares me. What if he does not look back after tonight, like Ramy didn't.

I adjust the strap of my wristwatch to divert my attention. I realize it is 9 p.m. already. Amid all the conversation, I lost track of time. Maybe that's what a joint does to you sometimes, and love on other occasions.

'You may continue to stargaze. I need to go, make arrangements for the campfire.'

'I will come along. I want to be of some help.'

We start walking towards the campsite, urging the locals to pile up some wood and make arrangements for the campfire.

'Do you know why a campfire is essential to the trek?'

'No,' he looks puzzled.

'Since times immemorial, humans have gathered around fire to share stories with each other. I have done this activity on previous treks too. When twenty-five strangers, who come from diverse backgrounds, share their stories, it is magical.'

'Sometimes, connecting with a stranger is far easier than connecting with our close ones. The conversation flows so effortlessly. Isn't it the strangest thing?'

'Just like I feel this sense of connection with you?' he says and leans towards me again. I push him back playfully.

DUSK TO DAWN

Kabir

Sunday, 1 January 2017
The Milky Kheerganga (2960 metres above sea level)
Parvati Valley, Kasol
Himachal Pradesh, India

'Don't try to fit in, accept yourself the way
you are.
If you feel that the cubicle isn't for you, build
some for others!'

Looks like, after months of doing the same thing, Myra has begun to do the tasks like reflexes. There is something about her that attracts me to her. She is so different from all the other girls her age. Living on her own and for such a long time must be difficult and challenging. She has been taking people for treks all by herself. It requires a lot of skill. How many of us can convince so many people to take the tough road? Do things the way we want them to do?

She has been doing all this and has succeeded in living independently. I am in awe of her.

Myra takes the lead as everyone sits around the campfire. 'You've got an opportunity to break free, to look beyond the cubicle walls and meet new people. Try to absorb as much as you can and make the most of the opportunity. I am sure you don't get a break often. Do you?' she asks.

'No,' everyone utters in unison.

'It does not matter who you are, where you've come from, or where you are headed. At this point in your life, this group will relate to you more than anyone else in this world. We share the sorrow of an ailing past and look forward to being able to pursue our dreams. All right, so let us start this activity by introducing ourselves and sharing why we are here.'

'Clockwise, from there,' she points to the girl in a violet dress.

'Hello, everyone. I am Veronika. I am here with my girlfriend, Natalie. We wish to travel the world together and that's why we are here! We met in Goa two years ago and instantly fell in love. I am from the Czech Republic and she is from New Zealand. We love India and keep coming back here because India teaches you to love others. You see, we Czechs get bored of our landlocked nation, so I have another reason to be visiting—the beaches.'

Everyone joins her in laughter.

'It's funny how you guys want to come back to the roots while we wish to fly away. The way our culture fascinates you, yours fascinates us!' a middle-aged man enthusiastically chimes.

'Hello everyone. I am Ted. I am from the US. I first came to India way back in the 1970s. The booking platforms and Internet have made it very easy to plan trips these days. When I travelled in the 1970s, it was very different. Currency exchange systems were not so user-friendly and quick. I travelled to Goa as a sixteen-year-old. There were a lot of Portuguese there then. I fell in love for the first time; made love under the stars with a Russian woman in her mid-thirties. I shall cherish those memories forever. I don't know what brings me here, to India, again and again. I think her blue eyes will hold me captive forever.'

Everybody smiles in amazement.

'Do you still love her?' asks a young girl.

'No questions,' Myra warns with a smile.

'Hello everyone! I am David. I am an investment banker in Israel. So, I have a huge bank balance, you see!' he laughs. 'I have taken early retirement to focus on things I did not do before, travel being the most important. India is the first country in my itinerary. I am headed to the South East next.'

'Hola! I am Amelie. I have always been a compulsive planner. I knew what I wanted out of each year, but did not know what I wanted from each moment. I saw a moving film and decided to walk out of my comfort zone. I am exploring and experimenting. I don't have plans any more. We're always busy planning the future, but unfortunately, we fail to live in the moment completely.'

Finally, it is the turn of the coy teenager in red pyjamas. 'I also wish to travel and explore the world just like everybody here. But I really can't! My family is not supportive. They tell me it is only for rich brats and hippies. This is my first trek. Nobody knows I am here. But for the first time in my life, I am not ashamed of being my true self,' she shares.

'You're very courageous,' I say.

'Hello everyone! My name is Ashray. I am on an all-India bicycle tour to raise awareness about entrepreneurship and encourage people to let their children take the tough road if they wish to.'

This guy gets a standing ovation from all the fellow travellers. He takes a little bow and is evidently happy.

After a few others, it is finally Myra's turn.

'I was employed as a software engineer, but I am travelling to figure out who I am. Travel has taught me to be humble and spread as much love as I can, because life is too short and our presence too temporary on a timeline that stretches beyond our imagination! The universe makes you feel small in front of the bigger plan which we are all part of.'

'Do you ever consider going back?' asks the young girl.

'No, my family will get me married in their quest to fix the broken person I have become.'

'Is it safe?'

'It is scary and definitely not very safe, but sometimes, you wish to go beyond these constraints to find your true self. Is it madness? Yes, it is. A little bit of madness is essential to live a full life.'

And then, she points at me. I want her to be as eager to know my story as I was to know hers.

'Hello everyone! I am Kabir. I am here with my friend Sandy. I don't know what brings me here, but here is what I will take back with me. The moment I gazed into the clear sky, I fell in love with the boundlessness of the universe. Suddenly, my problems felt minuscule. There is absolutely nothing more humbling than the silence of the hills and the sound of the ocean.'

'Hello, everyone! I am Sandy. I code, play the guitar, start up companies now and then. I write weird research papers. My latest research is on how music can transport you to places. If teleportation is possible, this is too. The world calls me crazy and I call the world crazy!' he says as he takes a long drag from the shrinking joint in his hand.

The weather changes all of a sudden. Cold bursts of wind assault our cheeks, and very soon, tiny snowflakes fall lightly over us. Myra instructs everyone to rush to their respective camps and turn on the heaters. We invite her to our tent. She comes without a second thought. Sandy is bent over his guitar, strumming to escort all of us to another level of existence.

'You may choose to stay back with us and work on the next big idea,' I prod Myra.

'No. I don't wish to.'

'I see the spark in you. I don't want you to lose that.'

'I don't see any sparks though,' she laughs.

'Whom do you think you are fighting this battle with?'

'Sorry?'

'You're headed towards loneliness, and I don't see it working for you. In dark times, our struggle is majorly with the self, not with the others, as it might seem.'

'So what do I do?'

'Let's take this trek as an example. People present here might see this as a gateway to their new, improved lives. Everybody has felt that at some point in their life, I think. This trek might help them decide what is right and what is wrong, or maybe what they wish to do in their lives, but this does not nurture them or groom them to be able to do that. Entrepreneurship can't be preached to people, it is something which has to be practised by them, patiently and intently. That's the way I see the light at the end of the tunnel. Sandy and I wish to bring that change.'

'I am not sure of anything yet!'

'You can choose to walk back to the city where your parents will get you married and "your own" weekend would be about drinking and buying expensive passes to stand-up comedy shows just to laugh once in a week!'

Everything I say should make sense to her.

'I do have an idea, but I don't really have a team. I have spent two months trying to figure out what exactly to do next. I failed miserably, and then realized that sometimes, the force lies in the team and not in the individual.'

After an hour of dialogue and negotiation, she gives in. 'Yes, I want to work on the next big idea!'

'Don't try to fit in, accept yourself the way you are. If you feel the cubicle isn't for you, build some for others!'

Travel has ignited a fire in me, which I believe, is here to stay.

START-UP IDEAS

Myra

January 2017
The Beatles Ashram
Rishikesh, Uttarakhand, India

'Never judge someone by who they are today,
but who they can become tomorrow.'

A million thoughts swirl in my head at any moment. But when I ride a bike on the highway, witnessing the countryside pass by, I feel free from those iterative thoughts, and practically everything else. My mind becomes a blank slate until yet another thought paints it in its colour. Sometimes, we all crave for that little space called thoughtlessness. As a child, I used to believe that as we move ahead, the backdrop moves along with us. But as a grown up, I certainly know that what is gone is left behind forever, and there is only one way, the one that lies ahead.

We have covered 400 km in the last three days. How? Sleepless nights, a continuous bike ride, unfaltering support for each other, empty pockets, and eyes full of dreams. Ramy's Redemption Roadmap rule number 1 really works. No phone calls, no messages and no social media for some time makes everything around feel simply surreal.

We cross a milestone that reads, Rishikesh: 89 km.

After a few minutes, I realize I had fallen asleep while riding pillion. Kabir shakes me repeatedly to wake me up.

'Are you out of your mind?'

'What happened?' I say in a feeble tone. 'There could have been a major accident.'

'Seems as if she is sleeping after ages,' Sandy says with concern, 'Leave her alone.' He pulls out a bottle of water from his bag and gives it to me.

I take small sips and nod. 'Will be careful,' I say. I am still unsure if I will be able to live up to my words.

Sandy hints at Kabir to stop on the side of the highway, gesticulating with his little finger. Kabir asks him in disdain, 'Company for the loo?'

I laugh, 'You may go! I don't mind.'

'Shut up and follow me,' Sandy commands and walks away without waiting for an answer. Kabir follows. Sandy has been acting a bit strange since morning. I overhear their conversation.

'We need to make stops more often,' Sandy says in a low voice.

'Let's get a bit practical about the situation.'

'For how long will the savings last?'

'Pooling everything, we have roughly 10K, so it should last for another week.'

'We will take up some part-time job. I can play the guitar,' Sandy laughs, 'You can wait tables.'

He scratches his chin, 'We can't do away with the necessities of life.'

'You're right, Sandy. You were never concerned about Karen. But, Myra . . . eh?'

'She is a good person. That's all!'

I pull out a fidget spinner from my rucksack and indulge in a little play. I hope it will keep me from falling asleep. As they walk back towards me, I add with a sigh, 'Since I left Mumbai, I have seen worse, been through worse.' I try to conceal my tears but my emotions reflect in my feeble voice.

'We'll be fine, guys. Chill!' Sandy assures.

'Where should we stay?' I ask.

Sandy almost jumps with joy, 'There is an ashram in Rishikesh. Steve Jobs stayed there thirty-five years ago when the idea of starting Apple hit him. He also suggested it to Mark Zuckerberg, who then visited the place four years ago. We're headed there.'

Actually, Sandy and Kabir have gone a step further in idolizing their start-up role models. They desire to walk exactly in their footsteps and do things as naive as imaginable to become like them.

'Guys! Stop daydreaming. That ashram is near Nainital!'

'Why the hell are we here in Rishikesh then?' Sandy yells in frustration as he looks at Kabir.

'I am sorry, Sandy. I thought it was in Rishikesh.' Kabir confesses.

Sandy angrily kicks a stone lying in front of him 'Thought?' he can't stop himself from raising his voice.

'I am sorry, guys. I don't know why I absent-mindedly believed it was here.'

At times, you fail miserably at trusting your instinct, especially on the highway. 'We can't drive to Nainital now. I have an idea though. We can stay at the Beatles Ashram. They offer boarding facility in one of their newly constructed hostels. The good news is that we can save big bucks on food and lodging,' I say.

Sandy turns towards Kabir with a weird expression and says almost cynically, 'Set Beatles Ashram as the next location on your iPad.'

The Beatles Ashram stands tall on the banks of the holy Ganga. Ganga is famous for karmic cleansing among Hindus. It has washed off so many sins that it has itself turned into a gutter of the modern human civilization. The yogi who managed this ashram passed away long ago, but has left behind a legacy—that of transcendental meditation. The Beatles visited the ashram in 1968 to study transcendental meditation, hence the name.

We register ourselves at the reception and are issued a week's stay pass.

'Would you like to volunteer?' asks the skinny old sage at the desk.

'For?'

'*Seva*. Selfless service?'

'Yes,' Sandy commits.

'All three?'

'Yes!' we add due to obligation.

'In that case, the cost of your food and stay will be waived off. You can reclaim it before leaving. Present yourselves at 9 a.m. and indulge in seva activities for two hours then on.'

We nod.

'Am I clear?' he quips, in a rather curt tone, an eyebrow raised. The scepticism conveys that many people commit but fail to deliver.

'Yes.' 'Yes.' 'Yes.' We say, one after the other.

We walk around the ashram to acquaint ourselves with the serene place. Most of it looks like remains from World War II. Parts that have been built anew house people seeking wisdom under the guidance of the disciples of the yogi. The older buildings are built in the shape of dome-like caves that overlook the Ganga. The most famous meditation cave, number nine, is believed to be John Lennon's.

We decide to sit in cave number nine and brainstorm for the coming days. An artist has painted a graffiti inside, in red, yellow, blue and green, to convey, 'It is all in the mind,' to the unapologetic society. People often pass by such pieces of art and call the artists crazy. Yes, they are crazy enough to believe that they can change mindsets. Even crazier to paint their hearts out on rocks like these.

As I look at the graffiti, I realize, 'Maybe, Ramy is not the crazy one, the rest of us are.'

Kabir starts, 'We should come up with an idea in the housing and rental space. A lot of bachelors in the ages between twenty and thirty find it difficult to get a nice apartment in metro cities. You see guys. This is a real-time problem that we can solve.'

I counter, 'How do we partner with landlords? We are ourselves in that age group. Why should they trust us or our ideas for that matter?'

'Unless we have some USP.'

'We can't charge higher rentals for sure. What else could be the bait for landlords?'

Consider: Sandy laughs, 'Unless the landlord is desperate!'

I look at him with a poker face. 'Why would he be?'

'If there is some problem with the house itself?'

'Why would a person want to move into a house that has infrastructural problems?'

'What if the problem is not infrastructural? What if the house is haunted, or ran a sex racket?'

I can't believe Sandy at times. 'Woah! So you want us to create an online marketplace of haunted houses and brothels.'

We laugh and laugh until we are in tears. We rummage through more ideas—setting up a cafe chain across India, samosa chain, managing food deliveries and groceries even. Most of the day goes by, but we make no headway. By evening, Sandy gets philosophical after smoking marijuana and so do I. After chatting for hours, we decide to head back to our rooms.

The next day, I ask Sandy, 'What are the kind of apps that you've created?'

'Most of them were games on android. I have mastered gaming and animation. But smartphone games are more short-lived. You don't really need to establish a company or have a specific business model for that.'

Kabir adds, 'He has been doing it since college. He would sit in the library or lab for hours, bunking class, creating apps. He is a whiz at coding. Once we have an idea in place, he will take care of everything else.'

'What was your idea, Kabir? The one you suggested during the trek? Let us forget the constraints for a minute. What if we merge the idea of The Redemption Trails with your idea? If we could convince the investors, what's the deal then?'

'Convincing the investors without having any experience of starting up is the biggest deal,' Sandy frowns.

'Let's think of some real-time problems that people face in their day-to-day lives and try to solve that first,' Kabir maintains his stance.

Sandy suggests some mobility issues. I counter them with some scope in virtual reality, Artificial Intelligence, SaaS products and mobility.

'E-commerce?'

'E-commerce is flooded already.'

'What if we could solve some real-time problems for companies through gaming. I have relevant experience too.'

We debate and ideate, but unfortunately, the sun sets yet again and we are unable to reach a conclusion. Finally, all of us float in the Himalayas, eyes searching for a reflection of ourselves in the universe above. I don't like marijuana as much as the company it allows me to enjoy. I don't smoke for the heck of it. I smoke for the wonderful break it gives me. I feel like I am in a metamorphosis of my own: from a stone that sat in front of a computer and coded all day into a sponge that absorbs knowledge.

Ramy is right, travel leads to the re-engineering of one's mind. Whenever you have a problem, try to enlarge your perspective, look at the sky and the stars. I want an intoxication that lasts longer. Longer than alcohol, longer than weed and longer than drugs. That intoxication should come from their passion for work.

Never judge someone by who they are today, but who they can become tomorrow.

BIRTH OF THE BRAINCHILD

Kabir

January, 2017
The Beatles Ashram
Rishikesh, Uttarakhand, India

'Some of the greatest start-up ideas lie in the trash bins of cafes.'

I step out of my cave and cannot help but appreciate the hues of the evening sky. A woman meditates in the corner-most cave, number 18. I feel captivated by the aura of optimism and exuberance around her. She is wearing a saffron robe painted with 'Om' in charcoal grey. In no time, I find myself seated next to her. She must be in her mid-fifties, charming and elegant, with deep blue eyes and golden hair.

I don't want her to freak out. 'I am Kabir,' I slightly bend, my hands together to wish her, 'Namaste.'

'Suki,' she replies and folds her hands too.

'May I sit here for a while?'

'Of course, son!'

After years, I hear the word son. Her words cause a tiny teardrop to roll down my right cheek. I feel as if she holds an inexplicable power over me. Like she owns me. Sandy's mother is the closest I have come to feel a mother's love. Nothing is absolute. Not even right and wrong. The wrong always feels right, and the right feels like an obligation. But mother's love is all giving, forgiving and unreasonably absolute.

But men are not supposed to cry. Are they? I have mastered the art of wiping my tears with the finesse of a serial killer, leaving no trace behind. The temporary marks on my shirt are proof that some truths are hard to conceal, at least at the moment, before they evaporate. I am brave enough to survive without my mother, I reassure myself, once again.

'For how long have you been here?' I ask her.

'Four years!'

'Four years?' She smiles.

'Can I ask you something?' I say hesitantly.

'Ask me whatever you wish to!'

'Don't you feel bored here?'

She laughs, 'It sounds boring to young people, but this is my life, and I have chosen it to be this way. I have lived my life to the fullest before practising sannyas. I used to seek knowledge about others earlier, now I wish to know about myself.'

'Your family?'

'My kids are your age now. They're doing well in their lives. My ex-husband is a rich businessman settled in London.'

'I am sorry!'

'Don't be. There is no bitterness involved. We loved each other immensely. I eloped at the age of nineteen. With time, our priorities changed; he wanted money, and I wanted much more than that. To be honest, neither of us is wrong. It's just that our goals and hence paths are different.'

'Does true love happen only once?'

'When you say,' she stresses on the words, 'only once,' and then continues in a soft tone, 'you put a constraint on love. But love knows no constraints. It happens with life. We fall in love. We fall out of love. Then, we fall in love again. Change is the only constant.'

When I was with Karen, I thought I was in love. She could not mend the broken bridge that was our relationship when we walked it together. She stayed there. So I crossed it alone. Now, I am here, on the other side, gone forever. On the calendar of life, a heartbreak marks the end of an era for some, but a new beginning for others.

'Are they your friends?' she points to an area behind me. I turn to see that Sandy and Myra are having a conversation in front of our cave. Myra's laughter is loud enough to be heard from a distance. I presume Sandy is cracking jokes.

'Yes!'

'What brings you here?'

'We are here to brainstorm the next big start-up idea,' I wink.

'You've come to the perfect place then,' she assures, 'but I wish to warn you!'

'Warn?'

'The longer you stay here, the more you will get to know yourself. At this juncture, you should be aware only to a certain extent to get back to the real world.'

'A week? Is a week enough to make us stay forever?'

'I can't comment on that, son.'

I can't live the life of a hermit. Not anytime soon. But I respect and value her words.

'Is concentrating on your breath in your free time the best way to meditate?'

'It is one of the ways to meditate, not the only way. Meditation is like identifying the music that your heart dances to and filtering out the background noise. Let's take your example. When you're working on something you love, you get lost in it after a while, don't you?'

'When I work on an idea, I put every effort into it.'

'When you work on what you love, it is like meditation. If each one of us does what we love and pours our heart and soul into it, we would not have to meditate elsewhere. The way I am doing it now, after years of not doing what I wanted to! Your work is like worshipping God, a journey to the self. The only satisfying journey that you will ever take. Not colour, not nation, not wealth, a person is known by his work and contribution to humankind as a whole.'

'What should keep us going? Wealth, fame or?' I stutter in doubt.

'None. The thirst for knowledge should keep you going. Since knowledge is infinite, there is no particular destination. Keep learning, every day, all the time, keep searching, keep looking.'

'What's the best way to resolve a conflict?'

'In the end, people who love you, and the purpose you've contributed to will make you happy. The option that aligns to this goal should be the best one in my opinion.'

'It is dinner time,' she suddenly says and gets up to leave.

She looks into my eyes, 'What is bothering you, son?'

'I feel deeply touched when you call me son,' I say with a sigh, 'my mother,' she interrupts me before I can pour my heart out, 'You can call me maa!'

She empathizes with the pain in my voice. She does not want me to cry again. Moved by her words, I say, 'Thanks,' and let out a sigh again, 'Maa!'

I don't blink until she disappears in the dark canopy of cedar trees on the path that leads to the central hall of the ashram. I gaze towards the dusking sky amid the silence of the Himalayas and the sound of the flowing Ganga. Suddenly, my problems seem minuscule. There is absolutely nothing like experiencing love. You feel bliss only when you let yourself loose in the empire of intangible possessions—experiences and memories.

Myra spends the night researching on my iPad so she can substantiate her stance on social entrepreneurship. Men often underestimate women, that's the most stupid thing we do!

The next morning, we go to the central hall for seva services. We have been asked to assemble an hour early today. The ashram trust has organized a monthly feast for the sages and the commoners.

The old man at the desk greets us and says, 'The duty hours have been extended to three hours today.'

He hands over a broom to Sandy, 'Clean the hall and align the rugs parallel to each other from this end to the other,' he points to the door.

Sandy frowns in disapproval. He gives in though. The old man instructs me, 'Come along and look after the registrations on the front desk.'

The central hall sits ensconced among the rest of the caves. As Myra and the other volunteers roll up the jute curtains, sunlight enlivens the room and the surrounding caves become visible. We are flanked by the valley on one side and the jungle on the other. The only sounds are of the chirping birds and the flowing river. I exchange smiles with fellow volunteers who have their reasons to commit to the challenging seva schedule.

The entry door to the hall, where I sit, is facing the valley. To work here is a different feeling altogether. Never in my life had I imagined doing something like this! These memories will stay with me even after I die. Our bodies might become a topic of research, but these stories, stories of love and humanity, will be passed on from one generation to the other. The more love we share, the more we help shape a loving world!

'Hey girl,' a *bhikshu* in orange robes turns restless and shouts at Myra, 'Get me another gulab jamun.' The serene environment of the ashram gets disturbed, all at once. Looks like he is tripping on a high dosage of marijuana, enough to make him hallucinate and lose temper.

She rushes to serve him two pieces. He grabs her by the wrist and warns, 'Run away. Run away. I asked you to run away.' She falls on her back in an effort to not tip over him. The aluminium bucket filled with gulab jamuns crashes to the ground, scattering the red balls dipped in syrup across the hall. Everybody stops eating and looks on in shock. Sandy and I rush to rescue her. The old man from the desk accompanies us.

I grab her by the waist and lift her up. 'Thank you,' she says and hugs me softly. She looks up at me tenderly, her eyes brimming with gratitude. The scandalous man, begging for attention, repeats, 'Ask her to leave.' She immediately runs towards the washroom. The moment he touched her, I felt the blood rush to my head. But I refrained from indulging in any action that could land us in trouble. The old man from the desk says,

'You guys may take care of the girl. We have a couple of other volunteers joining in.'

'Ok,' Sandy and I nod.

'Let's go back to the cave,' he suggests as we walk out of the hall.

'Sure.'

'Are you in love with her?' he teases. 'No. Just concerned.'

'Ten years.'

'What?'

'I have known you for ten years. You can lie to yourself, not me,' he says as he takes a joint out of his military print pants.

'Just concerned.'

'She will be all right.'

I freak out looking at the joint, 'Why did you buy it? We're broke!'

He lights the joint and passes it to me, 'Relax! I got it for free.'

'Free?'

'Weed rotates in Karmic cycles. If you give it to someone today, you get it back from someone else tomorrow,' he punches me in the belly playfully. We laugh.

I wish to meet Suki again. I want more answers from her. I visit her cave to realize she is practising silence for a month. Her face is calm, eyes closed and body in the state of ultimate bliss. I realize she was a part of my journey only for a few minutes. Yet, she left an impression that will stay for a lifetime. 'Maa,' I utter into the ears of the universe as I can't say it aloud. She smiles in her sleep. Some thoughts leave ripples in the fabric of the universe. They find refuge beyond the constraints of time and space.

We meet in cave number 9 yet again, hoping to finalize an idea. We make a temporary table by stacking three flat rocks on top of each other. Myra initiates the discussion for the first time.

Myra: I like cafes for their ability to bring everyone at one place and chat, bond, work. Cafes are where most revolutions have been ignited in history. In 1675, King Charles II banned cafes in England. Cafes barred women in France too!

Sandy: So, you want us to start a coffee chain? Cafes have inundated Indian markets. Competition is huge.

Kabir: Let her complete first!

Myra: If we wish to reach the youth, it has to be through the cafe culture. Cafes are where the new rebels will get inspiration from the old rebels.

Sandy: Rebel? But weren't we producing entrepreneurs until yesterday?

Kabir: Rebel, like some pioneer of the new technology age?

Sandy: Steve Jobs? Narayana Murthy? Mahatma Gandhi? Christopher Columbus? Are we going to change the world and become revolutionaries? What the fuck are you talking about?

Kabir: We can't change the world.

Myra: It is about the ideas that can change the world!

Kabir: Christopher Columbus was not the real discoverer of the Americas. Native Americans always knew that America existed. He opened a gate for the rest of the world.

Sandy: Followed by death and destruction of the natives.

Myra: Ok, I will rephrase it—ideas that can change the world for the greater good!

Kabir: Sounds better.

Myra: Cafes have become the new workplaces while offices have become free coffee stations!

Kabir: Most of the networking happens during coffee time.

Myra: Where do most of India's start-up ideas end up?

Sandy: Not in practice.

Kabir: I agree.

Myra: Think guys!

Me: Cafes?

Myra: You're close.

Sandy: Engineering colleges?

Myra: More guesses?

Sandy and I look at her with poker faces. Neither of us has a clue.

Myra: The trash bins of the cafes.

Sandy: Trash bins?

Myra: We scribble on tissues, in diaries and on scraps of paper, and before leaving the cafe, we throw them in the trash!

Kabir: Not because we lack belief in our idea, we lack belief in ourselves.

Myra: If we take up the initiative to collect these pieces of paper from trash bins and bring the ideas back to the table, we are indeed working for a better tomorrow.

Sandy: How do we do that?

Myra: Let us suppose, our vision is to create the next-generation of tech entrepreneurs from India. Who do we need for that?

Kabir: People with ideas.

Myra: But here's the catch. India does not lack people with ideas. It requires the right attitude.

Kabir: The social conditioning makes us risk-averse.

Myra: What if we create co-working spaces with mentorship in a place away from the city's hustle and bustle and grow into next-generation incubators as we scale up?

Sandy: I read an article on TechCrunch this morning. The future is in the sharing economy. We share cabs to get to our destinations. We don't wish to own apartments as much as the older generation did.

Kabir: On all trips abroad I have rented Airbnbs.

Myra: So when we can drive anywhere, stay anywhere, why can't we work from anywhere?

Kabir: A co-working space also gives the flexibility to work during weekends.

Sandy: This is more like an idea, creating a prototype is hard. Back in Silicon Valley, investors fund promising ideas, but in India, that is not the case.

Kabir: Plus, this will be high on investment. How do we make profits?

Myra: Don't go back to square one. It's simple because sharing economy is the future.

Sandy: Also, this sounds more like a social entrepreneurship thing. To produce entrepreneurs is the prime minister's problem, not ours.

Myra: You are highly mistaken then. The youth is the future of the country. We will determine the future of our children. The government can only support us. It is stupid to believe that the government can bring about a change on its own.

Sandy: These aspirations are too good to see the light of the day. I have been a part of a few failed start-up ideas before. You guys are completely unaware of the dark side, the investor politics and the other hanky-panky that goes on in the industry.

Kabir: Suki, the woman I spoke to yesterday, told me the advantage of helping others. I am partially biased towards Myra's idea.

Sandy: That crap? It's Newton's third law of motion in philosophy.

Kabir: Care to explain?

Sandy: Every action has an equal and opposite reaction. So what goes around, may, as well, come around.

Myra: Let's come back to the topic!

Sandy: You want us to establish co-working spaces?

Myra: The problem is, there are millions out there, especially women, who wish to pursue their idea, but what they lack is the right guidance and platform.

Sandy: How can we assume there are millions? Who did the maths?

Myra: Call any random number from your phonebook and ask. Ask if they've ever wanted to do something on their own? If yes, why have they not been able to?

Sandy: Well! Go ahead. Call ten people.

Myra: My phone has been switched off since I left Mumbai.

Kabir: Your family? Do they know you are here?

Myra: No.

Sandy: So who exactly knows you are here?

Myra: No one. Except for you guys.

Kabir: For how long will this go on?

Myra: I will buy a new connection once I start living in a city again.

Kabir: I don't wish to switch on my phone either. It is very peaceful without social media. I don't want my uncle or Karen to know anything about me.

Sandy: Looks like none of us have our phones on! Peace.

Myra: I floated an anonymous research survey among my colleagues. Five thousand IT professionals were part of the study. Fifty-five per cent of the respondents said that they would want to do something of their own once in their lives.

Kabir: We can conduct more such surveys once we are back in the city.

Myra: Many Indians were entrepreneurs before the Britishers brainwashed us into believing that we were not. The Indus Valley Civilization is proof that we were the pioneers of the underground sewage system. We've always had ideas. We grew our own cotton to make clothes. We made our own shoes.

Sandy: Unfortunately, now we only have the service class, which only mends shoes!

Kabir: Our GDP was a quarter of the global economy until the 1700s. Can you beat that?

Myra: It will work. We will bring about a change in the country's mindset and ecosystem. This is not an idea or a company. We will spark an entrepreneurial revolution. Not that I want everyone to become entrepreneurs, but to have a fearless attitude like entrepreneurs.

Sandy: If we don't make profits, we'll soon be dead. The sad part is debt follows even after death!

Kabir: There is no harm in trying. After all, that's all we can do.

At the end of our discussion, I switch on the screen of my iPad and notice an email pop-up from the world's largest start-up event, TechTalks—Pitch to Disrupt: Think you have the next big idea? The event venue is Hotel Phoenix, Barcelona.

Kabir: What if we get an opportunity to pitch at an event of such stature?

Myra: Seems like a dream.

Sandy: Guys, let's apply for TechTalks!

Myra: Yes. We will apply for a lot of events this year. Including our very own Start-up India, Stand Up India.

Sandy: Let's start with TechTalks. We need to get going. Otherwise, we will just keep discussing like we have been doing for a few days now. This will mark the start. Let's get the basic things right, the elevator pitch, the business model, the break-even analysis, the go-to-market strategy and the competition analysis!

Myra: But which idea are we going to pitch?

Kabir: Ummm . . .

Sandy: Your idea.

Myra: Are you convinced?

Sandy: Yeah! Let's give it a try. I have started up a couple of ventures. I am not afraid to give another one a try. We will make it work.

Kabir: What will be the name of the company?

Myra: Millennials Co-working Company.

Sandy: How did you come up with a name in an instant? Deciding a name takes up to a few months!

Myra: I have been thinking about this idea since college. Three years? Is three years a short time?

Kabir: Not at all. In fact, I like the name. MCC, we call it MCC.

Myra: Or MC^2?

Sandy: MC^2 sounds amazing! Even Einstein would love it! The energy of India $(E) = MC^2$.

Kabir: The entries for this year close within a few days.

Sandy: The clock is ticking, quite literally.

Myra: Where do we go next?

Kabir: We have neither time nor money.

Sandy: Gurugram houses a large number of start-ups. It is the closest to Rishikesh. Moreover, Kabir and I are well acquainted with the NCR region.

Myra: Let's start, team!

Kabir: Let's start, team!

Sandy: Let's start, team!

'World, we're coming,' we scream in unison, as we run out of the cave. The valley reverberates with the sound of our determination, of our energy and our dream. The world seems to dance around me. Never have I felt so complete before!

Irrespective of whether we make it big or not, this feeling of euphoria is a rare bliss in this world full of fleeting accomplishments. This day, our fate is sealed. This day, Millennials Co-working Company aka MC^2 is born.

A NEW HOPE

Myra

March 2017
Millennials Co-working Company
Gurugram, India

'Fridays or Mondays are not a big deal to me any more. When you love what you do, every day is like Sunday.'

A new place, a new home, yet again. After hitting the open road, I have not gone back home, not even once. The road has become my home and the people I have met my family. When I introspect on what I have become, my heart answers that I am a sum of all the people I have met on the open road, all the experiences I have had on the open road.

Across from me, the street looks like a never-ending train of automobiles, sans the pedestrians. I am standing in the balcony of my new office-cum-home 4BHK in Cyber City in Gurugram, which is replete with major corporates and luxury housing communities. Gurugram is not exactly a city. It is Delhi's adolescent offspring—sixteen-year-old, rash, abusive and impulsive. Showing off for him is next only to breathing, breathing dust! But who cares? After the Silicon Valley of India, Bengaluru, Gurugram houses a vast number of tech companies. It is the white gold city, lustrous with its IT and infrastructural pursuits, yet hollow at heart.

Gurugram is a large breeding ground for start-ups. While some start-ups achieve new heights, others stay put in blogs that go down in ranking on Google's search results as time passes. Our fate is yet to be determined!

Every day feels the same since I began working here. It does not matter if it is a Sunday or a Monday. When you leave a nine-to-five job, the concept of weekends disappears from your reality. I work day and night to make things work yet I never feel overworked. That's the beauty of loving what you do or doing what you love! I have never experienced this kind of peace or sense of belonging; not even at my own home, because home now means my idea, my people.

Sandy's network led us to Mr Kapoor, a trader who made it big in the 1990s. He values India's ever-changing technology landscape. At fifty-five, Kapoor has married his daughters to NRIs in Canada and Australia, respectively. He has a remarkable laugh, an open-hearted attitude and an undying passion for whiskey. Oh sorry! Single malts and cigars describe him better. He tells us that he has spent money on every possible thing, including the soaring real-estate and a world tour last year, but his bank account won't ever starve. So basically, his situation is the exact opposite of ours.

Our jaws dropped when we saw his apartment. I remember Sandy whispering, 'What better place than the white gold city to utilize one's black money?'

'Shut up, Sandy. He might open the door any moment,' I warned.

Kapoor warmly welcomed us in. It was a cold January night. Winters in Gurugram are gut-wrenching. I have to cover myself in double the clothing as compared to Kabir and Sandy to battle it.

As Kapoor spoke, we realized he was a survivor of demonetization that hit the country worse than a natural calamity last year in November. But, fortunately for us and unfortunately for the government, he had found out the best way to spend his extra money. He was willing to invest in us. And suddenly, we found our angel. Sorry! Angel investor.

'A place to live and work on our idea,' Kabir emphasized.

He handed over the keys to his empty apartment, 'You may have this until your first investment.'

Kabir cleared his throat and hesitantly asked, 'Rent?' Sandy and I crossed our fingers. We looked at him with our big eyes brimming with tears, exactly like the Japanese cartoon characters.

He kept a hand firmly on Kabir's shoulder and said, 'I am a businessman, I can see the future. Just allow me 2 per cent equity! You guys have the spark. You'll grow big soon!'

Now, I must tell you, Kapoor is far-sighted. He might not be as far-sighted as Elon Musk—eying Mars as the next address. But he understands the game of equity—of investing today and expecting returns tomorrow. He is not your regular boss who asks for an updated excel sheet every month end.

We are safe for a few months.

How can strangers have such overwhelming faith in us when our own families have disowned us? Anywhere in the world, to create an empire out of nothing, someone must have invested in someone else's idea. In life, you just need to have patience and find your own Kapoor!

Sandy breaks my line of thought as he steps into the balcony to hand me a cup of tea, 'Your relationship with your investor is like a marriage, it is a long-term commitment. So, we have to choose the guy wisely. Kapoor is fine, but we need a mentor!'

Soon, Kabir joins us. He strictly abides by his morning gym schedule. Sandy and I are the lazy ones!

'Kabir, brief us on the plan for this week.'

'The good news is that we have two investor line-ups this week. Today and Friday!'

So, this is the update.

We're looking for a mentor now. Someone who knows the industry inside out. Someone who can guide us with our dilemmas and show us the right path. We have listed ourselves on every possible website that promises to skyrocket your business idea overnight. The promise is like the ones made by fairness cream companies though! You know it is not going to happen overnight, but you fall for the trap.

RITEISH THELAWALA, BUSINESS PARTNER, THELAWALA AND COMPANY

While in the cab, we agree to let Sandy do most of the talking. Sandy is the most experienced of us all, and we don't want to take any risks with our first presentation.

We reach Thelawala and Company thirty minutes before the scheduled time, but are signalled to go in by a secretary exactly thirty minutes after the scheduled time. We wait for another hour, but we can still be deemed lucky. The average in the industry is more than an hour, and we have heard horror stories over beer at parties with some start-up co-founders who claimed to have waited for as long as eight hours! But, here's the catch. If you waited for sixteen hours for your IT company interview during campus placements, this is still a lot better!

Riteish is sitting on his big black leather chair, cross-legged, munching a samosa. His belly is meaty, round and looks huge enough for a breakfast buffet at a five-star hotel!

He greets us with a curt 'Hello guys' and offers us seats, his eyes fixed on the MacBook Pro in front of him. We take the seats opposite him.

The table is loaded with snacks, such as samosas, bread pakoras, parathas and tea, including ours. He gestures us to feel free to pick up anything from the table. We refrain to do that though, out of sheer courtesy.

'Tell me about yourself?'

Are we here for a fucking interview? A corporate interview like the ones that happen in campus placements where you are converted into a lie machine to safeguard yourself from other liars. Eventually, the biggest liar wins the battle.

'Umm. Should I start first?' Kabir asks politely.

'Yes, go ahead, what's stopping you?' he growls.

He still hasn't made eye contact and continues to type something on his MacBook; his left hand holding a samosa.

Sandy suggests, 'Sir! You may take your time if you're busy. We will wait for you!'

Riteish shuts the flap of the MacBook. He picks up another samosa and changes the course of the discussion, 'Do you know the difference between an accelerator and an incubator?'

Sandy volunteers, 'An incubator is . . . '

Riteish interrupts, 'Hold on. Who do you think we are?'

'Neither. You are an investor.'

'You've got this wrong, kiddo. We are an incubator.'

'Ok, Sir.'

'We are mentors, mentoring the star entrepreneurs of tomorrow!' he stresses.

Star entrepreneurs? This guy talks like a reality show host—flashy, dramatic and made-up.

I speak up for the very first time, 'How can you help us with our idea?'

'Lady, we will provide you the incubation.'

That's tricky. We're creating next-gen co-working spaces that are supposed to act as incubators. An incubator will incubate another! I don't wish to beat around the bush. I want to make another point, right here, right now. 'We are looking for investment.'

'We will connect you, not only to investors, but also to mentors.' So who is he? A middleman. The stories of exploitation by middlemen dates back to feudal days. We can't be fooled by him.

Sandy asks, 'What do you expect in return?'

'You just need to pay the fixed rentals for the infrastructure and give us a minimum stake of 8 per cent in your company.' He knows what he wants. This is the only thing I appreciate about him—he is straightforward.

'Eight per cent?' Kabir asks.

I know he is asking for way too much, but what option do you really have when you're broke?

'We can negotiate further provided you are interested.'

'Sir, we will get back to you in some time.'

'Sure.' He gestures to help ourselves to the snacks on the table. We follow his lead and pick up the tea cups in front of us, one after the other. A red dragon, exhaling fire, is printed on our mugs. I glance at the dragon, and then back at Riteish. I can't help but wonder whether the dragon on the cup is symbolic of the man in front of us; of the trap that might be waiting for us. Should we go with his proposal?

He notices me intently looking at the boastful cup and points to the dragon, 'I have businesses back in China and Hong Kong, you see!' With the air of an achiever, he adds, 'I am a global businessman.' The global businessman continues to gorge on the deep-fried desi samosas.

'You truly are!' I say with a smile.

There comes a point in every conversation when it can't be stretched any further. The situation is similar to the cafe meeting with your partner before a long-awaited break-up. Hours go by. He knows your story. You know his story. It is time to say bye-bye!

We stand up, shake hands and are about to leave the room when he breaks the lull with utmost sincerity, 'Please make the payment at the counter outside.'

'Sir, for?' Kabir says with some hesitation.

'I am a consultant, and I have invested my time in helping you out with your next move.'

Wait. Wait. Wait. Really? When the fuck did that happen? Free lunches? That does not happen any more.

Now, I wish I had picked up more than just tea. I could have grabbed a samosa or two.

'We will,' Sandy says and makes it obvious for us to not argue and move out. He pays Rs 5000 at the counter.

'Sandy, this is not justified!'

'We can't have a bad rapport with any of the investors until we've made it big. It's a close-knit community. They smoke cigars and attend parties together. We might as well get banned from their circle!'

We go back to the apartment without saying much. There is gloom all over. None of us speaks a word. Being broke is not a joke. It does not matter what's broke, your heart or your pocket. It hurts just the same!

PREMCHAND AGGARWAL/AGRAWAL/AGARWAL/ AGARWALA, OWNER, FUTURA OIL MILLS

Premchand's office is far from the city. How far? You have to take an auto, then the metro, then again an auto, and repeat it at least ten times, before you reach his office. People travel to Mecca from countries across the world in the name of God. It is their pilgrimage. After starting up a company, going to investors becomes your pilgrimage, and your company is your God.

Nevertheless, we make it in time. We can't afford to do otherwise. We are not celebrities yet! Believing that becoming a start-up co-founder elevates you to the status of a celebrity is sheer stupidity. Waiting for investors is often like waiting for a train on a railway station. It never arrives on time and when it accidentally does, it parks you on the outskirts to seek revenge.

It's worth giving entrepreneurship a try though. I have learnt three things today, even before meeting Premchand!

Kabir elaborates the idea. He has the spark of a CEO in his eyes. After all, he has pitched to clients across the world, sold diapers literally. Our idea is much more sophisticated, isn't it? His prior experience does give us an upper edge. Today, Sandy and I keep quiet!

Premchand listens to the idea with the tenacity of a trustworthy lover. The smile on his face makes it pretty evident that he likes the idea and might accept our proposal. Maybe today is the day when our prayers won't fall on deaf ears, and this will prove to be a successful pilgrimage.

After fifteen minutes of pitching, Premchand interrupts, 'You have made the product. But what next? You need to sell it. Right?'

'Yes.'

'How?'

'We have a plan in place.'

'What am I here for then?'

An investor's ego is as fragile as the male ego. When the guy has the money, you try not to hurt his feelings.

'I did not get you, Sir?'

'Believe me, Kabir,' he says with a piercing clarity in his eyes, 'even if I have to stand at the mall's entry gate with your product in my hands, I will do it.' He is the Bollywood-style lover who claims to never fall back on his promises. But this isn't a film, and lovers are known to betray even in films. Premchand is the ultimate lover, the one who promises togetherness and marriage. That seldom happens; weren't most of your ex-lovers faking love?

'Sir, but this is a co-working space!'

Yes. Kabir has a point. It is a co-working space. It is not a physical product that one can hold in their hands and sell. We are not planning to sell combs on the local trains of Mumbai! He didn't even listen to the presentation, or did he?

Everything about Premchand seemed perfectly fine until 'the promise' happened. The managerial gyan of international bestsellers sold on streets goes down the toilet the moment you hear this! The business magazines are a big lie too. A struggling entrepreneur had told me that once you get big, you can always pay the media to write inspiring articles on your start-up journey. So your mind tells you to read the offer document carefully before investing. So what if he is investing the money? You are going to invest time and effort. So we pack up and decide to never get back to Futura Oil Mills. Not in this lifetime! In life, the number of people who tell you it can't happen is drastically high as compared to the ones who tell you it CAN!

VYOM OBEROI A.K.A SERIAL ENTREPRENEUR, THE SILICON-VALLEY-RETURNED GLOBAL DESI

Through his LinkedIn profile, we find out that he has a master's degree from Stanford. He's looking for new talent—young entrepreneurs, reads his caption. He has started up a few companies back in the valley too. LinkedIn is the new game and Vyom has mastered it to the last bit. He shares his wisdom regularly, with young and lost people like us. He contacted us himself after discovering the pamphlets of Millennials Co-working Company. Where? So a few days ago, Sandy got high on marijuana and decided to code all night in the Chaayos 24x7 outlet. After ten cups of tea, two joints, and coding on his laptop for sixteen hours straight, he left the pamphlets of our start-up where he was sitting.

Vyom picked it up the next morning and was intrigued by the idea.

He called Kabir to fix a meeting. Sandy's debacle became our company's miracle. Do I believe in destiny? Of course, I do. Days before this happened, I bought posters from Connaught Place and pasted them all over our new office. One of them read, 'And, when you want something, all the universe conspires in helping you to achieve it—Paulo Coelho.'

Vyom has called us for a meeting at Onyx Cafe and Bar, Cyber City. I presume he is a cool guy for meeting us on a Friday evening. No more discussions over tea and coffee. This one is going to be over drinks, I suppose. Vyom could be the guy, our guy, who is going to make our dream come true. The idea of meeting in Onyx scares me though. My bank account has hit the lowest limit and I am being fined for that too—for being too poor, to be precise. I hope he pays the bill.

'You must be Sandeepan?' Vyom points to Sandy. The guy has done his homework well. While we were stalking him on LinkedIn, he was up to that too! How on earth did he know that Sandy was Sandeepan otherwise? Even his biological mother does not remember his real name.

'Yes, Sir!'

'Relax! Call me Vyom,' he says in an American accent. We share a laugh and pleasantries.

'I love your idea,' he says, 'drinks on me guys.' He is the first guy who has gone through our presentation. At least, he won't promise to stand at a mall's gate to sell our 'product'. So this guy, rich, polished and worthy of respect, looks like a potential convert.

'Ma'am, please have a seat,' he drags a chair for me and politely asks the guys to sit next to me. He draws a chair opposite us.

I receive a call from an unknown number. When you're networking in the business world, you never ignore a call. He could be your next client, even better, your next investor!

'Excuse me, guys.'

'Sure ma'am,' he smiles. Kabir and Sandy look at me with a puzzled look. They must be wondering why I have left such an important meeting. I walk out hesitantly.

'Hello'

'Hello, Ma'am!'

'Yes?'

'Would you like to sign up for a credit card. We have a lot of offers for entrepreneurs.'

'Ok. So, for once and for all, people should realize that not everyone who is an entrepreneur is super rich. Most of us are struggling to make things work. We respect your opinion, and therefore, you should respect this fact.'

'I am sorry, Ma'am, should I call you at some other time?'

'How are you so sure that I won't be broke by then?' I hang up on her. I regret being rude. But I can't take this shit any more. It is difficult to not lose your calm when nothing works out for days and days in a row. But I tell myself not to lose hope. The more people reject you and your idea, your will to prove them wrong becomes stronger. I walk back steadily, wiping off the last bit of stress from my face, and join them on the table with a firm smile—a fake smile.

'What would you like to have?' Vyom asks.

'Heineken,' says Sandy. 'Corona,' adds Kabir. 'A red wine sangria,' I say.

Wine has the worst effect on me. Worse than whiskey. Yet, I order wine. After months, I feel I deserve to enjoy as much as other people my age.

'Guys, isn't the music too loud here?' Vyom complains. 'Yeah, it is!'

He signals the waiter to lower the volume and subsequently places the order on our behalf. He orders a 'Glenfiddich' for himself and adds, 'Chicken steak, baked nachos and french fries!'

'What would you guys like to have?'

'That should be fine, Vyom.'

'Are you guys dating?' he points to Kabir and me.

'No,' we reply together and exchange confused looks.

'I am kidding, guys. Take it easy. Back in the valley, many co-founders start dating each other after a while!' he clarifies with a laugh.

'So tell me, what's your story?' He points to Sandy, 'You start!'

Sandy recounts how we met in Kheerganga two months ago and how our idea shaped up. A few glasses of wine, an empathetic investor, our start-up story, and idle chit-chat all around feel awesome!

I catch myself appreciating our journey—where we started and how far we have come; how we have overcome our fears. It seems surreal. We don't get time to think about this when we are working. Sometimes in life, we're so busy worrying about the future that we forget to sit back and think about all we have achieved so far. This conversation reaffirms our belief in ourselves as a team!

Meanwhile, the starters arrive. Vyom takes a small bite and screams, 'I'm fucked, Lord.' Everyone stops and stares at him. He grabs the water bottle lying in front of him and gulps the water thirstily. I am amazed, or rather amused by his behaviour.

He clarifies, 'Excuse me, guys! After returning from the valley, it is tough for me to ingest spicy food.' He calls the waiter and negotiates a replacement. He then takes a closer look at Sandy's tattoo and reads out loud, 'The oceans and the sky lie within.' He sighs, 'What does that mean?'

'Everything is in our mind.'

'You look like an interesting guy. I get a feeling you're a musician.'

'Yes.'

'What do you play?'

'I play the drums.'

'Woah! I was the lead guitarist of my band back in the day.'

Hours pass. Vyom and Sandy have found comfort in discussing their respective band's stories. Vyom sees his younger self in Sandy. He thinks Sandy can help him become the boy he used to be. It's all fine by me, as long as he is convinced enough to pour in some American dollars into our business.

We continue to gulp our drinks. Our idea and investment have taken a backseat now. Vyom is too drunk to handle. 'I am afraid I am going through a midlife crisis.' I don't have an answer to this. Neither am I a career counsellor nor a therapist. I won accolades for being the best employee and shit like that, but now I am nobody to guide him.

Kabir whispers, 'Let's take a walk outside.' I nod, 'Yes, sure.' There can't be a better time to exit the discussion. It will lead nowhere. A person in crisis can only provide some emotional support to another person in crisis. Rarely do they reach a practical solution that can be acted upon.

'Are you feeling all right?' Kabir asks me as we walk out of Onyx. The corridor is full of buzzing restaurants and bars. We're surrounded by the big corporate towers of Cyber City. A few others, who have decided to walk out of the party with their friends, pass us by.

'No Kabir, I don't feel good. How long? For how long should we wait before things start to work?' I break into tears. Despite lying to myself for days in a row, I realize I am feeling low, maybe depressed. Yes, I do realize I might be the weakest among the three of us.

'Look around and tell me who is happy?' He tries to cheer me up like he does every time I feel low.

'Everyone. Like every fucking person around me looks happy! What more do I say?'

'I did not ask: Who around you looks happy? I asked who do you think is happy?'

'How do I see that?'

'Take a closer look. Try to see beyond those smiling faces.'

He points to a group of young IT professionals walking out of the club next to Onyx, 'What do you see?'

'A bunch of guys having fun. What should I see?'

The guy in a black shirt in the group has got too drunk to take care of himself. He loses his balance and falls on his face. The beer bottle he was holding minutes ago shatters all around. He screams, 'I will fuck Monish. Bastard! He makes me work for eighteen hours. Screw him. Screw this company.' His friends support him, help him get up and carry him like a dead body.

'What do you think, Myra?'

'I would have felt the same had I not escaped Mumbai the day I understood this never-ending rat race was bound to take me nowhere!'

Next, Kabir points to a beautiful girl, dressed in a red dress and beige stilettos, who is walking faster than the guy who is apparently chasing her, requesting her to stay. 'Please, Avisha! Listen to me once.'

I chase Ramy just like this guy chases her. Every day. 'Nothing hurts more than unrequited love.'

Kabir looks into my eyes and says, 'Who knows this better than me?'

'Who are you in love with?'

'It baffles me that the person I love asks me this!'

He is drunk. He is not lying to me. Yes, I am sure he isn't. But there's a weird triangle, or maybe circle. I love Ramy.

Kabir loves me. And maybe, Karen still loves him. Only Sandy is the practical guy who keeps away from 'love' and focuses on 'marijuana' and his 'guitar' instead. He is just like Ramy—devoid of all human affections.

At least one aspect of your life should be sorted. Either your work life or your love life. But you see, your twenties is a weird maze, almost everything in your life moves at a random pace. A few glasses of wine make me realize what a few months of waiting never did. Ramy is a dream. A dream I have been chasing for way too long. But Kabir is my reality.

A reality I can feel, understand and fall back on. It didn't happen in Kheerganga, it didn't happen in the days that followed, but I know it will happen today. You somehow know minutes before it's going to happen!

I surrender myself—to his honesty; to his friendship; to the trust I have in him, which I could never have in Ramy; to the feeling of being single for too long; to the feeling of incompleteness I had in my troubled relationship with Siddharth. I surrender by closing my eyes so that Kabir knows I want him to kiss me, hold me, feel me, feel every inch of me, my soul, my existence.

The moment his lips brush against mine, I forget we're standing right in the middle of the corridor. The fear of others looking at me, judging me or talking about me magically vanishes. You know what's the best part of experiencing love? Love conquers fear. Love conquers doubt. Love conquers loneliness. Most of all, however, love conquers the deepest demons of your mind.

We kiss each other endlessly. As if everything we have ever wanted to tell each other has taken a different form, a different language, the universal language of love, understood by all. And when you can kiss, where is the need to speak? When you talk, you consciously hide a part of it. But when you kiss, can you lie? I can smell his perfume, taste his mouth, and feel his grip getting tighter around my waist. The tighter his hold gets, the lighter I feel. The pain dissolves in the mid-spring breeze brushing my hair.

He holds my hand and suggests we walk back to the apartment. The kiss triggers a chain of events that leads to us lying next to each other, naked, in a matter of thirty minutes. I don't want to escape deep relationships. There's peace you can't find alone, but you'll find it in that one person. Kabir is that person, that peace. But Ramy is chaos—the randomness I seek in my life.

I wake up like a blank slate after weeks and weeks of sleeplessness. I welcome the morning and make sandwiches for the three of us with inexplicable ease. To forgive Ramy and move on is nothing less than bliss. I feel on top of the world. I don't fear anything. There is a certain energy, hope and positivity that comes from within. It is the most special feeling. From now on, I may not deliver the best presentation, but I know, I will still be happy. I realize love is like a packet of cigarettes—self-destructing yet reassuring.

Sandy tells us that Vyom is not interested in investing in our idea. All he had wanted was company—broken people cling to other broken people. His last words were, 'I am sceptical to invest in Indian start-ups as the co-founders show lack of professionalism. They just want to make money for themselves and fire the employee force at large!'

Shit.

FAIL TO RISE

Kabir

March, 2017
Millennials Co-working Company
Gurugram, India

'The day you don't let others' opinion perturb you, you're on the way to greatness.'

I am unable to reach Ramy. Yes, I am searching for him. I don't want him to turn up one day. I somehow sense a connection between these two. What if Myra chooses to walk off with him? I would be devastated. I love her. I have felt love for the first time in my life, after years of dating girls I never loved, after years of missing a family. I don't want to lose her.

Sandy and I have become partners in crime. Your best friend never fails to put in an effort when it comes to wooing the woman you love. But, unfortunately, it is impossible to reach out to the nomad. Myra is absolutely correct. He does not keep in touch with anyone or leave a single clue about his whereabouts as he travels around the globe. He has not posted on his blog too. The last one was when we were in Kheerganga. His fans have posted messages and comments on his last blog, requesting him to return. So, it isn't just me who is looking for him, it's a whole bunch of us, chasing after him.

Every morning, I wake up to a rejection email or, worse, complete silence from investors. It is not a nice feeling. No matter what you do, rejection does not spare you! You are bound to face it, in projects, ventures, love and life. Even a job seeker has to wait for months before he can find a potential employer. Walking away from anything in life, your dream or your love, is the easiest thing to do. But to stay resolute, to hold on, to wait for the sunrise is difficult.

I decided to embrace the difficult the day I put in my papers at my company. How can I turn back now? I have decided to wait. Although, rejection rips off a layer of my skin every day. Yet, every day, I put on my favourite suit and prepare myself to pitch to an investor. I get rejected, dragged out, blocked. How can rejection be good, if at all? I have finally found an answer. Rejection lights a fire greater than acceptance. Isn't life all about keeping the fire alive? So I promise myself to keep burning, keep moving. If today is not my day, tomorrow has to be mine. I will make sure it does!

Luckily, Kapoor continues to have faith in us. Kapoor's ex-partner, Raghuram, is back from London. He has agreed to talk to us on Kapoor's request. I am hopeful. Hopeful that he is the guy who will melt our problems away with a magic wand. Hopeful that everything will fall into place as narrated in bedtime stories by grannies.

RAGHURAM IYER, RETIRED TRADER-TURNED-ANGEL INVESTOR, WORKS FROM HOME

A well-suited man in his late forties, Raghuram has a background in finance. He is the guy who reads every newspaper, mostly the pink kind. I am not presuming this. I see a bunch of them peeping out of his Louis Vuitton leather handbag. Newspapers in the era of blogs? He is a typical conservative guy who has decided not to move ahead with time. How can tech start-ups be of any interest to him? I wonder, but try to free my mind of any prejudice.

'To have an idea is one thing, but to make it work is a different ball game altogether,' he says. His voice is assertive, curt and domineering.

'Millennials Co-working Company aims to solve this problem for others. We want to help others pursue their idea,' Sandy pitches.

'How much do you think I should invest?' he asks.

Now, this is straightforward. Pretty much. This guy has cut out the crap. He does not want to know our struggle story. Nor does he wish to interview us. I keep quiet for a while. So does Sandy. So does Myra.

'What's the range you're looking at?' I don't want to ask for more than he has to offer. It might just land us in trouble. Not quoting a figure, at times, shows you're not prepared.

'Wait. Here's the plan. First, let me see how capable you are and then accordingly I will invest later on. Get me some clients and initial revenue. In five days. Yes, five.'

'Ok,' Myra replies.

'Every Tom, Dick and Harry wishes to start a company. Every fourth person travelling in the metro wants to become the next Mark Zuckerberg. Last week, I visited a Delhi University college. I was shocked to see young women aspiring to become entrepreneurs. Women can't drive straight, how can they head global ventures? Funny, yeah?'

Myra, for obvious reasons, frowns at his comment. She walks out of the room silently. I know that Raghu is not right, but do I have an option to disagree? Maybe, yes. Maybe, no. Maybe, yes. Maybe, no. Actually, no. Just then, Myra rushes back into the room. She sits in front of Raghuram, points at the laptop screen and asks, 'Who is she?'

'What's the point?'

'Just tell me! Who is she?'

'I don't know.'

'She is the co-founder of TechTalks Foundation. She organizes an event on a global scale. She encourages young people, like my team, to pursue entrepreneurship.'

Raghu realizes he has dragged himself into trouble by questioning women leaders in front of our team that comprises a woman. He pushes his chair back in an instant, picks up his bag and suggests, 'This is not worth my time. I have to rush for another meeting. I will give you a call back should I wish to talk to you guys!'

I know he is pretending to leave. He has time, a lot of it. But sometimes in life, it gets difficult to stay true to one's own words. Often ego consumes us, forcing us to take irrational decisions. Ego not only stunts our mental development, it also acts as a roadblock to love, acceptance and humanity.

'Let him go! We will find someone else,' Myra says with a smile. Sandy and I are stunned by the fact that the meeting had lasted less than two minutes. Even sex lasts longer!

Kapoor's help Raju, visits our office minutes after Raghuram leaves. He helps us with cleaning, washing and basic maintenance of the apartment. He walks up to me and asks, 'Are you sure you want Raghuram?'

'Raju, I don't have an option. I need to generate initial revenues. What if we get a chance to pitch in Barcelona? Do you even know where Barcelona is?'

'I just know Alipore and Delhi. I don't know where Barcelona is! But what I know is, I don't want you to end up like the guys before you.'

'I am confused! What are you trying to say?'

'Have you heard of At Your Door?'

'Yes. The start-up that shut shop last year?'

'Yes. You're not the first one in this apartment. This was their office. Raghuram was their investor.

Initially things were fine, but then he started interfering in the company's private matters, and, eventually, it led to a huge fight between the co-founders. Rohit Sir became an alcoholic and later got booked for a hit-and-run case. I don't want something similar to happen to you. You are good people. I want you to stay.'

They succumbed because of the pressure Raghu put on them? But the media reported otherwise! Well, I trust Raju more than the media. Just after one meeting, I can see that there is something wrong with him. Maybe, it is an intuition, a gut feeling. Sometimes, you've got to trust your instincts in life. They might not be entirely untrue. Raju might be illiterate, but in life, you need experience more than education!

ANURAG GUPTA, ASSOCIATE, LION INTERNATIONAL CORP.; WORKS FROM INTERNATIONAL AIRPORT LOUNGES, STARBUCKS AND FIVE-STAR HOTELS

After another fifteen days of no luck, I receive an email that promises to change our lives forever; that promises to show us the light, the path to success. It mentions that our B-Plan has been shortlisted from India. We're the only entry from our country. 'Guys, our B-plan has been shortlisted for TechTalks!' I announce to my broken-hearted team.

'That's great news,' Sandy screams as he rushes to the laptop to read the email out loud. 'Draft an email to the global investment firm Lion International Corp. They cannot overlook our idea now!' he tells me.

Three days later, Anurag Gupta, the company's associate, calls me for a meeting to JW Marriott. As usual, I make it there well in time. I walk into a French-style restaurant on the ground floor of the hotel. I remember visiting this place a year ago to meet a Chinese client. I managed to sell the highest number of diapers in a single meeting that day! I hope luck favours me this time as well. What startles me is that so much has changed in a matter of months. What motivates me is the belief that so much is about to change!

'Hey! Anurag.' Anurag has a warm smile. It is impossible to spot even a speck on his flawless white shirt, deep blue pants and tan leather shoes. He is the perfectly groomed corporate eye candy you can't help notice.

'Hi!'

'Congratulations, buddy! Ready to rock TechTalks 2017?' 'Thanks, Anurag! The answer to your question lies in your approval!'

We share a laugh. We order everything French as we talk everything Indian. I tell him our story. He tells me about his elaborate experience with the major global firm, the clients he meets, the deals he has brought in, and his phenomenal rise from an

Airtel sim card salesman to the senior associate at Lion International Corp.

There are so many success stories waiting to be told to the world. Everyone is struggling—an entrepreneur to raise his first investment, an employee to switch to a better role, a single mother to raise her child, an artist to pay the bills, some for a meal a day, and the list goes on! To think we are the only ones is foolish. However, amid all the chaos, the bliss is in sharing stories and paving the way for a better tomorrow for each one of us.

After a two-hour heart-to-heart, Anurag says, 'Our company likes your idea. But they believe you could have focused more on the draft of cash flows.'

'We'll work on it.'

'Cool, then. We can take things further as soon as the basic documentation is in place.'

'Anurag, what is the advice you give to co-founders?'

'Don't fall for the allure of money and fame. It takes months or years to achieve commendable success. You don't want to risk that for anything else. Do you?'

'I did not quite get you?'

'If you limit the definition of success to the amount of funding you raise or to the fame you get through media mentions, you'll soon lose track and make mistakes. Everything is temporary in this world. The fame, the mentions, the success. Some founders successfully exit while some lose much more than they have earned. The world of technology is ever-changing. Don't ever forget your purpose. You stepped into this uncomfortable zone, to help others, to build a better community, to change the world through your idea. Don't ever forget that!'

'What you are saying makes sense to me. I will remember every bit of it.'

I miss Suki today. She might be in Nepal by now. After Suki, I feel a fantastic connection with Anurag. In life, conversations flow so effortlessly with some people!

'That's good!'

'Do you think Lion International Corp. will invest in us?'

'I can't assure you of that. But what I can assure you of is that I will put my best foot forward. I am bowled over by your idea to help others pursue their passion and want it to see the light of the day. How many of us are actually doing what we wanted to? I wanted to be a movie director. I don't want other movie directors to become associate partners! We should all strive to become the best version of ourselves, our best selves!'

When you are a few pegs down, the words come straight from the heart. You know the other person is not lying. You can see it in their choice of words. And I get the feeling that he wants us to succeed.

He loses his balance as he tries to get up, 'Who is all-knowing, Kabir?'

'You.'

'No.'

'God is!'

'In the times of the Internet, Google is!' he jokes as he hits the ground.

I glance at my watch. It is 1 a.m. already. I book an Ola cab and wish him a happy journey for his flight to Bangalore. He jokes, 'Kabir, remember, good ventures like good orgasms take time to build up!'

'I will remember that, Anurag!' I laugh.

I rest my head against the window of the cab and look outside. It's been three months since I first left Delhi on my bike. But so much has changed. My perspectives, my worldview, my thoughts, my fears. I would not have grown to become the person I am today had I not decided to leave everything that day, had I not decided to hit the open road! The best way to overcome all of your fears is to realize them. You are scared of missing a train only till you miss one. Once it is gone, you start weighing your options. Life does not stop. It goes on. So why not miss the train and buy tickets to the next one? Maybe, this will lead you to your destination. And what if it does not? The world is a vast platform and opportunities are like trains, passing us by.

Everything seems good about today. I go to the balcony of our apartment-cum-office and light a Dunhill. My phone vibrates. It's Karen. I decide not to pick it up. What will I talk to her about?

Five minutes later, I give up and answer, 'Hello!'

'Hi, Kabir! I love you. Please come back to me.'

She sounds drunk. I can tell she is drunk. After all, I have known her since college. I feel guilty. I can't say anything to console her. I don't love her any more. And she has to move on. It is the worst feeling to know your ex has not moved on yet.

'Are you drunk?' I politely ask her.

'Yes,' she confesses in a broken voice.

'Karen, try to move on in life like I have. My venture means everything to me now. I don't want to get into the mess of relationships.'

'Don't lie to me. You're dating her! You're dating your co- founder!'

'What the heck? Who tells you all these cooked-up stories?'

'Kabir, I saw you kissing her in Cyber City last month. I could not believe my eyes. I decided to never talk to you about this. But it bothers me.'

I hang up as I realize two more things about life. First, when you're in love, suddenly the world becomes too small, and people you haven't met in months get news about you. Two, in the time of social media, and in the presence of a large number of social media stalkers, having a private life is a far-fetched dream. You might walk away from someone's life, but rarely do they walk away from yours.

***

SWAMI NATH, FOODZILLA BEVERAGES COMPANY, SILICON VALLEY OF INDIA—BANGALORE

Just a week is left before the last date to confirm our participation in TechTalks. Anurag has not replied yet. I ping him on WhatsApp to meet up in Bangalore, but he does not reply. He is a busy man!

So, ideally, I have this one last meeting before the deadline. The strange part, however, is that Swami has called me, only me! The only thing that matters is that he is our last hope!

I take the metro to the New Delhi railway station. I book a sleeper coach seat on the last train to Bangalore. Yes, in a matter of three months my lifestyle has been reduced to this, and I used to travel only business class. But I feel much more empowered at heart. Yes, you should realize your greatest fears! They can be anything from diving deep into the ocean to living the life you never imagined. Nothing empowers you more!

The night is full of anxiety and encounters with the harsh realities of life. Right next to me, on the floor of the coach, a woman is sitting with a newborn in her arms. I had heard about the other side of life, but never experienced it. My dad was rich, and growing up that was my only identity. But now, I have discovered a new self!

I remember Anurag and Suki's words: Don't ever forget, why you started this in the first place. You want to impact lives, you want to make a difference. I smile at the woman sitting next to me. I can't do anything else at this point. I am helpless too. But if my idea works, I can create ventures, I can create entrepreneurs, who will bring back more resources to my country. I feel reassured relying on the fact that I am going to impact many such lives. Yes, this is my vision, clearer than ever now.

Thoughts, thoughts and more thoughts. This feels like the longest night of my life.

The morning is a bright and sunny one in Bangalore. I peep out of the door of the train compartment and feel the breeze caress my very existence. I promise myself to not give up. This is the first time I am going to pitch to someone without the fear of getting rejected. If I don't make it to TechTalks this year, I will try my luck next year again. Yes, I will keep trying, I promise myself. I wash my face hunched over a rusty basin at the station and chew four gums on the way to Rajveer Villa—Swami's lavish abode in Indira Nagar.

A butler escorts me to the visitors' room. Rajveer Villa is like one of those huge havelis in old Bollywood films, the ones that quintessentially house a huge staircase covered in velvety red carpets. His beverages company has revolutionized the market by introducing new flavours that no one has heard of! From Aam Panna to Jamun Delight, he has experimented with every Indian flavour. And yes, his experiments have paid off in the form of a lavish, larger- than-life lifestyle.

'I hope you did not have any difficulty in reaching here?' Swami asks with a warm smile.

'No, Sir. Everyone around knows the exact address of your place.'

'Yes. Everybody knows and respects me. In life you need to earn respect. Only money gets you respect.'

I do not quite agree with his statement. I respect teachers, philosophers, writers, scientists and change-makers. They are not always the richest people of the world. But, it's their work, their contribution that gets them respect. I have become a yes-man though. I have been silenced by the opinions of the old and the rude. I can't protest. When you have your dreams at stake, you often learn to ignore people's opinion.

'What would you like to have? Tea, coffee, juice?'

'Coffee.'

'I think you should have some juice. My company is about to launch four new flavours this month. You're lucky to be among the ones who get to taste it early.'

Swami signals his butler to get us juice. He obeys his master and gets two glasses. One for him, one for me.

He points to a picture on his silver iPhone, 'What do you see?'

'Your family,' I reply.

'What else?'

'You look happy together. Looks like a picture from a vacation.'

'You are a fool! This is Oberoi Udaivilas.'

'I did not quite notice that, Sir!'

'Young boy! You still have a long way to go to be able to notice all things great.'

'Yes, Sir.'

'How is it?'

'Beautiful, Sir. It looks like a wonderful property.'

'Idiot! How's the new flavour? The juice?'

'It is great, Sir. Refreshing.'

He takes a sip, with his usual air of arrogance, 'What's your vision, Kabir?'

'I want to make a difference.'

'Profits. Your true vision has to be around money. Either you make money or you die. There is nothing in between.'

'Yes, Sir.'

'Have you ever asked yourself why you are failing again and again?'

'No.'

'You need to change your approach. You need to focus on money and profits. Get big fast. Focus on profits. There is nothing like "purpose". Save those terms for media interviews. Change your concept from social entrepreneurship to hard-core money-making entrepreneurship. You will see the results much sooner. Then, you won't have to meet people in those torn shoes.'

I am so lost in everything else that I have forgotten how I look. This has become so immaterial to me. Yes, I am the same guy who turned heads everywhere I went. Suki's words have come true. I have found a true purpose, a true reason for my existence. A vision that pulls me, work that entices me. Something that makes me forget the rest of the world. His words should have pinched me, should have hurt my ego, but surprisingly, I have become strong enough to let this slide. I realize that the day you don't let others' opinion perturb you, you're on your way to greatness. The idea of life isn't to change others, it is to make yourself so capable that external events do not affect you, and you become all accepting.

After a pause, he resumes, 'How can I afford a lavish Bungalow in Indira Nagar, the Beverly Hills of the Indian Silicon Valley?'

I am clueless, and I believe staying silent at this point makes more sense than arguing. I pretend to relish the juice, waiting for him to start talking again.

'Because I don't give a shit about social entrepreneurship!' he says.

'Yes, Sir.'

'I have a lot of start-up ideas that you have neither heard of nor would you be in a position to pursue.'

'Yes, Sir.'

'Do you know what my idea of life is?'

'Yes, Sir,' I say and then realize I was so lost in saying yes that I was not listening to what he was saying.

'No, Sir,' I clarify.

He is so hell-bent on flattering his ego that he does not even notice my mistake. Good for me!

'If you want someone to swim, just throw them in water, never ever do the spoon-feeding,' he suggests.

'Yes, Sir.'

The butler returns. But this time with another glass of juice. Ink blue juice! Yes, these monster juices exist and you thought blue ink was only meant for ballpoint pens. I hope it does not taste awful! This guy would not let me say no. He places two glasses in front of us. One for him. One for me.

Swami leans in towards me and says in a low tone, 'Now, let's talk about your idea!'

'Millennials Co-working Company aims to,' I begin but he interrupts me, rather screams in excitement, 'Actually, it is one of the most innovative and exciting ideas I have come across in weeks.'

I let out a sigh of relief. I hope he was just dramatizing the whole situation, maybe it was his way of breaking the ice! 'So are you willing to invest, Sir?' I say with the frivolousness of a kid buying an orange candy.

'Yes.' He takes a sip from his glass, 'How's it?'

'It's like a dream come true. I am glad you liked our idea.'

'No. No. No. How's the juice?'

'Good!'

'Just good?'

'Great, Sir.'

Shit. Shit. Shit. This guy is obsessed with himself and 'his juice'. It tastes like shit. But what option do I have? I want to pick up the glass and throw the juice on his white clothes!

'Now tell me, what were you saying?'

'Are you willing to invest in our idea?'

'No. Not yet. I want you to change your vision first, kiddo! Take your time. You can let me know anytime before the TechTalks deadline. I hope you will take the right decision and fly to Barcelona!'

He forcibly takes me on a guided tour of his bungalow. He has paintings by artists I have never heard of and shoes of brands I once used to own. In life, I have come across all sorts of people, but never someone with such braggadocio!

We take a walk to his balcony, a part of which has been developed as the club's outer area, where he smokes cigarettes and hukkah and shows off.

He pulls out a cigarette from his pocket. Oh God! I don't like to smoke with just anyone. This is the worst thing that could have happened today. Smoking with someone I can't connect with is like making love to a woman I don't like. Yes, it's as terrible as that!

He takes a drag and offers it to me. I take it reluctantly. At times, life throws lemons at you, big ones, unripe ones, that hit you like stones one after the other. I offer the last part of the cigarette to him, not to show respect but to avoid smoking his cigarette.

People say, this too shall pass. Yes, those are the exact words iterating in my head. I start thinking the misery is about to end, but the butler returns. The green of his new juice is deeper than Pakistan's flag itself. Will I be spared on nationalist grounds? No. The answer is no. I drink the third glass of juice within twenty minutes.

'Have you heard of Mount Carmel Hills, Mussoorie?'

'Yes, Sir. My father and uncle attended high school there.

Do your children study in Mount Carmel?'

'No. I am your uncle's batchmate. I have called you here on his request.'

'Oh! I am happy to know he is willing to help me!'

'Idiot! I am here to make sure you don't make it to TechTalks! Two days to go before the deadline. I wish you all the best!'

I walk out feeling uneasy and helpless! It is always good to be in the company of people who are better than you as they help you grow. It might sound tricky, but I realize it is good to meet a few shallow people now and then. At times, criticism creates greater ripples than support. Also, you get to know who you don't want to become.

I call Sandy. I can't call Myra. I am afraid she will lose her calm. I narrate the shit that happened in the exact order of events, and, as expected, Sandy keeps his calm intact, as intact as the board on the exit gate of Rajveer Villa that reads, 'BEWARE OF DOG'.

Sandy says, 'If there are multiple universes, chances are that in some other universe we would travel to Barcelona and win the event! So cheer up!'

'This is too filmi, Sandy. Stop feeding so much Hollywood sci-fi to your head. Bloody, how do you manage to look at the brighter side always! Love you, dude.'

'Walk back to the station. Board the first train back to Delhi. We'll figure out a way!'

Yes, sometimes, it is a matter of chance—to be at the wrong place at the wrong time. Today, I learn a few more things about life. First, knowing who you don't want to become is equally important as knowing who you want to become. Second, your relatives and family can prove to be impediments to your success, like in my case. Just like those films we have grown up watching, where the villains pull out every dirty trick in their bag and cause trouble.

RAMY RETURNS

Myra

April, 2017
Millennials Co-working Company
Gurugram, India

'Life proves to be one hell of a ride. All you've
got to believe is that the things that do not
work out lead to the ones that do! As the
journey goes on, there's a lot more to learn!'

I decide to laze around, the way we do after weeks and weeks of working hard. I wallow on the sofa, reading other start-up stories on HerSaga. It has become my only dose of inspiration. At times I feel like the glass that shatters into a million pieces, which can never be brought back to its original shape. Buddy flashes an unknown number. I am not sure who it is! After three unanswered calls, I pick up.

'Hello!'

'Hello.'

'Beta, I am Sandy's mom.'

'Yes, Aunty! Is Sandy's phone unreachable?'

'No, beta. I wanted to talk to you.'

'Yes.'

'I am like your mother. If you face any problem, or if you feel like visiting home, you're always welcome at our place.'

'Thanks.'

'The journey is full of ups and downs. Avoid the prejudice that everybody is bad and nobody is going to help. I am sure God will make way for you guys, I know you are meant to shine bright. All the best for the competition.'

'Thanks, Aunty. Thanks for your support.' 'Mention not, beta!'

My Facebook is filled with messages from home, from people I have left behind. I wish I could talk to them, at least hear my mother's voice once. I love them, of course, I do. But they will never support my decisions. I fear that if they do not accept me, I may feel more heartbroken. Or, even worse, they might get me married.

Sandy will be out cashing the last of his contacts today, to convince at least one guy to come on board.

As I continue to browse on the Internet, I don't realize when I venture into the arena of uninspiring from inspiring.

I read a few articles:

Ask4Deal fires 500 employees, saw its employee expenses more than double to 737cr in a year from 268 cr. The founders have taken a 100% salary cut.

RentVillas shuts shop.

Is the IT bubble burst a reality in India? Massive layoffs in major companies.

Woah! Start-ups in the country are witnessing a rise and fall like a playful dolphin in an ocean of spectators. So are others! Unfortunately, what happens in the country affects us too.

Raghuram, yes this guy is Raghuram, smiles back with his half-broken front teeth from the picture. I recognize every square inch of his face. I click the link open that redirects me to a LinkedIn post by him! It reads: 'I am glad to announce that after a long break from the Indian market I am back with a new team. Meet Ajay, Rahul and Piyush, the co-founders of The Co-workers Commune, a next-generation co-working place for artists, entrepreneurs, writers and designers.'

An idea similar to ours? It can't be a coincidence. And, an all-male team, it is not a coincidence for sure!

A few minutes later, Anurag calls. I cross my fingers. At this juncture, that's all I can do!

'Hello, Myra?'

'Hi, Anurag!'

'Kabir's number is unreachable!'

'Oh yeah! He is in Bangalore. He was trying to reach out to you!'

'I am sorry, guys. I have been keeping busy lately.'

'I did not want you guys to keep anticipating the outcome of our evaluation. I am sorry to be so late to inform you, but, unfortunately, our firm is sceptical about investing in a social entrepreneurship initiative at this point in time. They have selected another B-plan from Singapore. I hope to see you in Barcelona. I am just an employee. I tried my best. That's all I could do!'

'Thanks, Anurag! It's ok. We're aggressively looking out for options. I hope we meet in Barcelona.'

I try to reach Kabir. But his phone is unreachable. Sandy does not respond either! While Kabir could be on the train, Sandy must be in a meeting.

And then, the most unexpected thing happens. Ramy calls. Something I have been terrified of. I don't wish to speak to him. I am angry, very angry. Why is he calling me now? How can he do this to me all the time? Abandon me when I need him the most and come back when I don't need him any more. I want to move on with my life. Do great things. Become the next big tech entrepreneur. To fall in love with him, all over again, is the last thing I want. But the moment he approaches me, I surrender to him. I do things he wants me to do. After moments of indecisive thoughts, I hesitantly pick up.

'Hello, Myra!'

'Hi.'

'How have you been, Myra? I hope all is well.'

'No. It isn't. Guess what, Ramy? I am close, very close to my destination. I have finally become an entrepreneur. My B-plan has been selected for TechTalks in Barcelona. But we don't have anyone backing us up from India. Nor do we have money to support our stay. It is just two days away. If we lose this chance, I have no clue for how long I will have to wait until such an opportunity knocks again. Everything is messed up. Why are you calling now, though?'

'You have no control over events external to you. But your inner self should not be disturbed. I always tell you to build yourself on the inside.'

'Ramy, I have to tell you something. Maybe, you'll never call me back after hearing this.'

'What?'

'I think I am in love.'

'With yourself?'

'Yes, and Kabir too. I have decided to move on. I am grateful you left me alone when it mattered the most. I could move on finally. I hope it does not bother you.'

'Why should it? I am very happy for you. I always wanted you to find the right guy. I believe Kabir is the right choice for you.'

'How do you know that? You have not met him yet!'

'I know you, more than you know yourself.'

'Ok then. That's it for now. I don't want to talk to you any more. It might not be the best thing for my future.'

'Yes. I don't have any qualms. Just follow my last advice.'

'What?'

'You know you've tried every possible way to reach out to people for help. But as the deadline nears, with every passing second, your chances of pitching in Barcelona become more bleak.'

'So what do I do?'

'Leverage the power of social media.'

'How?'

'Write an open letter.'

'To whom?'

'To the prime minister of India.'

'Have you gone crazy!'

'No, I have not.'

'So?'

'Don't be afraid! Just have faith in yourself. If you don't believe in your idea and initiative, why would anybody else?'

I feel nervous. Cold hands, cold feet. I break into a sweat. I don't even like to be in the limelight. Social media? It's like a monster. I loathe it unlike many from my generation. The point is that I am not so confident doing this.

'Ramy, I think we should talk later.'

'Don't hang up on me, Myra! Listen to me very carefully. Do as I say. Pick up your laptop and start typing. There are a few things that no school in the world can teach you. You have to figure out stuff on your own as you move forward in life. Have the courage to challenge the norms. Mario has to fight all by himself against all odds by living life on the edge to finally meet the princess. Even the video game is a manifestation of real life.'

'Wake up,' I open my eyes to see Kabir and Sandy. I must have fallen asleep on the sofa. 'What have you done, Myra?' Kabir yells at me. I get a feeling that I have done something awful. Like literally awful! But what have I done? I remember browsing the Internet and talking to people on the phone, and then Ramy called, and then I fell asleep. Has Ramy come back? Oh no! That can't happen. That should not happen. He does not know my address. He drags my laptop in front of me and points at a post on social media shared from our company's blog.

'Whose idea is this? I thought we were a team and it was important to have mutual consent before taking such a huge step?' Kabir yells. Sandy seems calm and collected. He has my laptop though. And he is browsing through our company's website. He is glued to the screen, unwilling to move or talk to me.

'Have I done something?' I ask, in the most innocuous way.

'Something is too vague to describe what you have done!' Sandy exclaims. He is not very upset with me. He is smiling mischievously. What could that smile mean? It's hard to tell yet.

'Myra, you've written an open letter to the PMO! Not personally, but from the company's blog! You've majorly highlighted the adversities involved in starting up and lack of real-time support from the bodies that claim to promote entrepreneurs! You've shared our real experiences! The only thing that saves us from facing more problems is the fact that you have not mentioned their real names!'

'She has done the right thing! We did not have any other option to reach out to the ones at the helm,' Sandy says and points at the screen in front of him. I get off the couch, slip into my flip-flops and push a reluctant Kabir aside to have a look.

'I don't remember anything! I don't remember typing a single word.'

Kabir does not seem convinced.

Sandy calls us to the main hall, yet again!

'Look at this,' he points at the screen and continues, 'Start-up India, Stand-up India's official twitter handle has retweeted this letter. And, do you know what the good news is? The blog is trending like wildfire across the Internet. Have a look at the analytics. So many start-up founders have shared it on their official social media account!'

Three days later, we are called to the office of Start-up India, Stand-up India. Our message and idea are lauded by the flag-bearers of entrepreneurship. This day our fate is sealed, yet again. This day Millennials Co-working Company is truly born!

The problem with the world is, nobody appreciates your idea or plan. But once you're live on TV, newspapers or the social media, suddenly your idea, and of course you, get credibility like no other. The good or the bad thing about social media is that it is not confined to your country. If the news spreads, it spreads across the world. Oh yes! Our inbox is flooded with 'All the Best' messages now. In the time of smartphones, all you need is one viral message to touch millions.

As I pack my bags to fly to Barcelona, I receive a message from my ex-boss, Arun. It reads, 'All the best!'

I reply, 'Thank you, Sir.' To forgive people and move on is always a difficult choice. But I guess, in the end, it is all worth it, and it is the best choice.

My letter has reached not just Mumbai, but the United States as well! Saurabh has also messaged me. He tells me that his H1B Visa has been denied and he plans to come back to India. He also wishes to become a part of our team.

Kabir comes to the hall and says, 'Guys! All set? I am booking a cab to the airport!'

'Yes, bro! All set,' Sandy is way too excited. He is travelling out of India for the first time. So am I! I love to travel. Travel is the only reason for my existence. Travel is what drives me. Travel is what makes me the person I am!

Kapoor visits our office just before we leave to motivate us, 'Guys, put your heart and soul into this endeavour. I always saw the spark in your eyes. It is time to reach for the stars,' he says as he bids us adieu.

As we get off at Indira Gandhi International Airport, I smile at the driver, overwhelmed. 'You're very courteous and well-behaved.' He truly deserves a five-star rating. It feels good to see how some start-up ideas are empowering people from all walks of life. I recall how Kashyap always said that real companies are the ones that touch people's everyday lives and help them evolve. They build India through enterprise!

Life, like entrepreneurship, is one hell of a ride. All you've got to believe is that the things that do not work out lead to the ones that do. This is what I have learnt so far, but as the journey goes on, there's a lot more to learn!

LIFE IS A JOURNEY

Kabir

April 2017
TechTalks Barcelona

'There has to be something, a person or
endeavour, that you can call yours in this life!

You're certainly lucky if you have both.'

I am standing atop a 500-feet-tall building, one of the many architectural wonders from the post-industrialization era, situated on the mesmerizing seafront of Barcelona. It is a luxury hotel. The kind that the traveller in each one of us admires on Facebook. I've been awarded a free stay though! This feels surreal. Yes, after months of setbacks, we have finally made it to the world's most coveted start-up event, TechTalks, Barcelona.

My partners-in-crime, Sandy and Myra, are standing on either side, stupefied by the view through the magnificent glass windows. We gaze at the horizon with high hopes and optimism as the blue of the morning sky mingles with the blue of the ocean. 'I have come a long way to beat the Monday blues,' Myra sighs.

Barcelona is not very different from Mumbai; it has a similar kind of architecture, there is a bizarre sense of freedom in the air, people walk on the streets in slippers at any time of the day, and a cool breeze blows perennially. Except summers in Europe mean longer days, much longer than Mumbai. Also, unlike Barcelona, Mumbai has a lot more skyscrapers.

Ramy once posted: Travelling West takes you to the future, travelling East takes you back to your roots. I envy him for being so close to Myra's heart, but I have to agree with him on this. After all, he is an expert when it comes to travel. No one understands the soul of a place better than he. He's a rare traveller in a world full of tourists, tourists like me!

'I had never imagined I would stay in a business suite,' Sandy confesses. 'This is just the beginning of all things great,' he adds.

'The wind at such a great height is strong enough to sweep one off their feet. You get the true feel of it while camping in the mountains. This glass window view is not for the faint-hearted,' Myra laughs.

I continue to sip my morning Americano as I nod. 'Sometimes I feel we can fly to the point we lay our eyes on! At other times I feel we will fall to the ground barefaced!'

'We will at least fly, in either scenario, and that is all that matters. Welcome to the world of start-ups. Nothing is predictable here,' Sandy asserts. He looks crazy in a white bathrobe though!

Every day has been like standing on one such point since the day we began nurturing our dream.

Just like the wind, every embrace of life brings with it a mix of feelings. Anything can happen, anytime. But that's the thrill of leading a turbulent life! Isn't it?

Today is one such windy day that will decide our course on the sands of time. If Millennials Co-working Company is embraced by the stalwarts of the tech start-up world, it will mark our entry into yet another phase of life.

We are as shapeless as water while alone, but together we are a small part of the bigger picture, an indispensable part of the universe, a wave of change. We're the co-founders of Millennials Coworking Company and our vision is to build India through entrepreneurship! Too ambitious? Yes, everybody, including our friends and family thought so!

Unfortunately, a lot of start-up ideas in India lie dumped in the trash cans of cafes. We scribble and scratch on tissue papers before we throw them away, the echo of the discussions doesn't even cross the walls of the cafe! 'You can't pursue entrepreneurship'—these are not mere words. This is an utterance of impending doom into the ears of the universe that convinces us to never pursue our dream.

But we are among the very few who have made it till here at the age of twenty-four, amid all the stalwarts of the business world, who will scrutinize our idea, and those of our competitors from across the world, down to the last detail. The journey was a roller-coaster ride. How could I expect it to be any different today?

'Let's suit up guys! It's showtime,' Myra says with a smile.

A lady in a sexy maroon dress announces the commencement of TechTalks. She is wearing a big name tag that reads Sheryl. The tag that sets our boundaries and determines our day at work, that makes us believe we can never innovate and are tied to our past decisions forever . . .

'TechTalks—Pitch to Disrupt is a unique event. Spectators from across the world, keep your eyes peeled as this could be your chance to make a mark in the tech biz. A live podcast is also available for those who want to watch the show. Every participant will be given one minute to share their vision and story. Subsequently, they will be judged on the basis of the answers they will give to the five questions asked by the panellists. Our panellists are from top investment firms across the globe and the sponsor TechTalks Foundation!'

'Irrespective of whether we win or lose, we can always hit the open road on a bike. Maybe to Amsterdam. Hash brownies have always been on my wish list,' Sandy tries to ease the pressure. He wants us to keep calm and believe in ourselves.

'You have said this over a hundred times in the last week!' I say. Myra is too stressed to be talking, I guess!

Each participant comes and conquers the stage. They all have some things in common—the energy, the fire, the passion! Entrepreneurs never fail to impress with their storytelling. Finally, after twenty-five teams, it is our turn to get on the stage. When the spotlight is on you, you realize, as the saying goes, you are prepared yet unprepared. My heart is pounding, throat feels scratchy and hands are ice-cold.

I breathe in a good amount of air, close my eyes for a second and tell myself, just believe in yourself, in my head.

'The industrialization, and then the digital age, has made us just like a programmed computer. Most of us are like the laptops we work on. We have some predefined codes which we execute. The idea of leaving our comfort nest and starting up is like a bug that hits the computer. Our society acts like the antivirus and dutifully clears the bug out of our mind. But when the bug starts to attack again, every now and then, like it did to us, the antivirus fails. We wish to challenge the antivirus in the system, and let our viruses thrive, to become entrepreneurs, leaders and change-makers. I wish to create a better future for our children, and our vision is to make tomorrow's India an entrepreneurial India.'

Sandy adds, 'We aspire to build a co-working space—a next-generation incubator that will give people the creative freedom to think away from the madness of the new metropolitans. For people to be able to break free from their constrained cubicle life and pursue new ideas, ideas that could have an impact, ideas that could change the world. As in most cases, breaking free from where one is stuck becomes much harder and therefore we give up on our ideas, our dreams.'

Sandy looks at me and continues confidently, 'We've known each other since school. We worked on a waste management project in seventh standard. That's how long we have been associated in our never-ending quest to create something new.'

Myra adds, 'Social entrepreneurship is something that excites us. Being a woman, in India, I know what women entrepreneurs go through and without the right guidance, it seems impossible to be able to reach our goals.'

Today, I learn that a story is as important as the way it is told. If you believe in your idea, others will definitely believe in it! Always tell the story, the true one, in which you believe!

'How was it?' Myra asks in excitement.

'The audience and the judges looked happy, but you can never be sure till the results are announced,' Sandy says.

A middle-aged man approaches Myra, and pats her on the back, 'Look how far you have come! I always told you to believe in your abilities a bit more!'

Myra squeals with delight. 'You were supposed to be in Europe!'

He laughs out loud. 'Where do you think Barcelona is?'

'Oh yes!'

'But you were supposed to be in the US, Myra. What about the on-site assignment?'

'Oh! Mr Kashyap. It is a long, long story,' she exclaims.

Myra introduces Mr Kashyap to us as an old acquaintance from Mumbai. He tells us how fantastic our presentation was, and that we do have a shot at winning as we undoubtedly won hearts, to say the least.

I ask Sandy to accompany Myra to the hall where the grand dinner is being hosted by the sponsors. I decide to linger around for a little longer and have a word with Mr Kashyap. After months of knowing Myra, this is the first time I have got to meet someone from her past. Maybe he knows Myra's best friend.

'Hello!'

'Hello again!'

'For how long have you known Myra?'

'A year I guess,' he smiles.

'I don't know where to start, but actually, I wanted to know about her best friend, Ramy. I have been chasing him for too long now. Do you know him or have you met him?'

'No. You won't either!'

'Why do you say so?'

'Because in my opinion, there is no one called Ramy!'

'Sorry, I did not get you!'

'When Myra was in Mumbai, she was depressed and was on prescription pills. It is around that time she started to mention this friend of hers to me. You see, she has a psychological condition called Multiple Personality Disorder. Ramy is none other than a split identity which takes over her when her depression is at its peak. Ramy's personality is her way of living life the way she wishes to. It is her defence mechanism that again and again resurfaces as a male alter ego because she believes women can't be entrepreneurs in this society.'

'That's crazy! I can't believe this. Everybody knows Ramy. We follow him on social media. Everybody knows he is a blogger.'

'Has anybody seen him? Has he ever posted a photo?'

'No.'

He takes out a piece of paper from his wallet and scribbles 'MYRA' on it. Then, he asks me to rearrange the letters and make as many words as possible. He hands over the pen to me. He watches me struggle.

ARMY AMRY RYAM RAMY

'Yes, that's it! There you go!'

He pats my back and explains, 'Most of us have our own Ramy. Our Ramy is the positive voice that hopes to save us from our demons. I do not know the sufferings of Myra's past, but she has made her split personality her best friend during depression. Now, it's your responsibility to make her face the truth and help her cope with it. You are in love with her, aren't you?'

'Yes. I am! Her blog, *On the Open Road*, gave me the courage to live my dreams. I owe this life to her! I can't thank you enough, Mr Kashyap! You've made my day!'

I rush to Sandy, confused, flushed, yet excited. Knowing that there is no Ramy gives me a sense of peace, a feeling of satisfaction, a new hope! Love is selfish as much as it is selfless.

'Sandy, there is no Ramy, and never was!'

'What the heck? I know they are serving free drinks, but don't overdo anything. We need to behave like professionals here,' he warns as he clears his throat and adjusts his tie in the most pretentious manner!

'You know how to hack into computers, right?'

'Yes. But wait? That's not right.'

'Chuck right or wrong! Just do as I say.'

I take him back to our hotel room, though not without some persuasion and force, and ask him to hack into Myra's laptop. Together, we trace her journey back to the day she left Mumbai. We find hidden folders, saved passwords and drafts of incomplete blogs, a series of evidence that confirms Kashyap's words. An incomplete poem on her laptop reads,

Alternate Reality
I breathe in and breathe out far away from the
maddening crowd.
  The tranquil sound of the universe around
transports me to somewhere beyond the blue
mountains and the green valley, to a different time,
a different alley.
  There, I meet Ramy.
  He looks like me and talks like me but sings in
the car and dances in the sea. He is everything I ever
wanted to be, everything I lost on the way.
  Yet, he is everything I want to become!

Three hours later, it is time for the results! We stand,
the three of us, holding each other's hands. I don't
know what Myra and Sandy are thinking right now.

I should be scared. Really scared. But I guess it
was scarier when I started out on my own. Now, it
seems I have made peace with the struggle. It defines
me. I don't wish to walk away from it now. I have
understood that the journey to success is a daunting
one, but it is the journey that matters. To be able
to live your dream you have to hit the open road,
someday. You have to give up everything and believe
in your dream. The destination might or might not
be as rewarding! Life can get tough at times, but the
journey leaves everlasting impressions, and hence one
must learn to appreciate it.

Sheryl announces, 'The winner is,' my heart skips a beat, 'The Home Guard.' Yes, it is hard to cope with the feeling of losing when you're almost at the destination. But then she continues, 'Accompanied by the Millennials Coworking Company, in the social entrepreneurship category.'

We laugh. We cry. I have never experienced tears of joy! I kiss Myra. We scream in unison, our voices stronger than ever. We run up to the stage and accept the prize. I realize that I have come a long way. We all have come a very long way.

'Where do you wish to travel next?' I ask our own Ramy, Myra. I want her to know that she will be his shadow until the day she looks into the mirror and discovers the rainbow within. There has to be something, a person or an endeavour, that you can call yours in this life! I certainly feel lucky to have both.

'Paris,' she confirms.

I want her to see what I can see. Aren't all of us living a version of us that we can't otherwise? Bravehearts like Myra are the ones who do! I will help her see the braveheart within her. My resolution is stronger than ever.

'Dude, I guess we're celebrating in Paris then,' Sandy screams with tears of joy as he hugs me.

As I check my phone, I can't believe my eyes. Start-up India, Stand-up India's official Twitter handle, has congratulated us on the victory!

Oh my God! The other news is that Swami has been booked for insider trading. I hope he does not poison the inmates with his juices!

The journey of life is not for the faint-hearted, it is equivalent to climbing the Everest. The most successful people are not the most talented ones, but the stronger ones who keep at it and do everything to realize their dreams. The dreams that would otherwise dissipate away into the wish lists on our screens or lie dead in the coffee shop trash bins.

EPILOGUE

Six months later

'Isn't she an inspiration?' marvels a young girl, one of the many assembled at Ignite, Women Entrepreneurship Summit, an event organized for aspiring women entrepreneurs.

'Whenever she posts on LinkedIn, I ardently wish that someday I am able to start a company of my own,' replies the one sitting next to her.

Myra slowly walks forward from the wings and on to the stage, with all eyes and the spotlight on her. Her voice booms in the hall which is full of bubbling aspirants, 'We, at Millennials Coworking Company, share a vision, the vision of making tomorrow's India, an entrepreneurial India.'

There is a great deal of cheering as the hall echoes with a thunderous applause.

She continues, 'I had almost decided to marry my boyfriend of eight years, and settle down in the US. I loved him more than anything, but I soon realized that getting married was not the sole aim of my life or the only way to live a fulfilling one—the way I was taught growing up in a middle-class family. I wanted to travel the world, but long before we could start travelling together, we had to part ways. I had to move on in life so my entrepreneurial dreams could see the light of day!

'In the absence of any support, I turned towards travel and decided to hit the open road. I finally found myself somewhere in the Himalayas, in the grasslands of Bengal, on the shores of Andamans, in the backwaters of Kerala, in the meadows of Bandhavgarh and in the forests of Assam.'

'Are you planning to start up a company because most of the content on websites and social media platforms makes it sound cool? The reality is very different. Let your inner self pull you, don't let the media and flashy stories push you. There's nothing worse than being at the wrong place for a wrong reason. You're sure to commit a big blunder in that scenario. Therefore, I never step back from sharing my true story. I want people to learn from my experience and be empowered to take difficult decisions on their own. It is true that people need to know the issues involved in starting up. It is not a rosy picture as painted by the social media. Yes, it's all true. I was depressed and lost for days before spotting the light.'

She then says with a chuckle, 'I believe you should know fifty reasons why you should not start a venture to be able to take a clear stand!

'There are many excuses to abandon your dream—a dearth of financial backing, lack of belief in yourself, etc. Society will tell you, don't feed the demons of your mind. Take suggestions from the angels in your life. Until the penultimate semester of your college, these supposed angels are your very own cousins, working or studying abroad. But as the final semester approaches, the upper hand is of college deans who herd you towards placements. Talking of demons—to fail at anything is considered the supreme demon in India. We are not completely at fault either. We were born in the post-colonial period when subjugation was not a restraint, but had become an attitude. I hope the Indian youth appreciate the true value of Independence and building India through enterprise.

'While the tales of courage and bravery are going around, let me tell you, I was the biggest coward, yet the only thing I could do well was find a way to be courageous. My mentor, Mr Kashyap, also the founder of Traveller's Nest, told me that your problem is not 'they', but 'you'. Find who 'you' want to become! Remember, your battle is as much with the self as with society. Girls, embrace your true selves. Love yourself. Have faith in your vision. Don't suppress the "girl" in you as girls can do wonders if they want to. The philosophy of life you should bank on is never to stop dreaming. Keep moving.'

As Myra ends with these words, I can feel her eyes brimming with the purest sense of pride. It is a great honour and indeed is very humbling to stand in front of a thousand dreaming girls as a role model and a mentor to be followed. My eyes are welling up too, as I rise to clap for the woman I have come to stand with and appreciate for her strength. I am joined by every single woman in attendance, every heart that Myra has inspired tonight with her honesty and ambition. As she walks down the stairs and reaches for my embrace, I can hear my heart swell with sheer happiness.

I know it in my heart that it wasn't easy for Myra. We spent months seeking psychotherapy. Mental health issues can haunt one for life if not tackled the right way. We worked on our dream throughout and although it did help her cope, she might never recover from it fully. But I will be with her, always . . .

The night comes to a close, but it is only a beginning for Myra, Sandy and me. What we have ignited within us took us a lot of soul-searching and months of agonised planning, and we seek to make it easier for the fellows on the same path as us. If only every single struggling entrepreneur kept believing in herself or himself, we have pledged to create an enabling, nourishing space for them to grow in. The journey begins with surrendering to yourself and your abilities first and keeping the doubts away—everything falls into place if only you give your everything to it!

FEELING INSPIRED?

MAKE A MOVE. Start your journey into the remarkable today.

Do give my other books *You Only Live Once* and *Where the Sun Never Sets* a read. I promise that they will inspire you as much as this one.

Please leave a review on Amazon/Flipkart/Goodreads. It will help me reach out to more readers who can be inspired to touch people's lives with their ideas!

If you'd like, also share your thoughts on social media using #stutichangle, #SCFamily.

ACKNOWLEDGEMENTS

To the beautiful gift of life and the journey we take.

To the days we wake up to nothingness, talk to ourselves, find hope delusional, haunted by loneliness, encumbered by shattered dreams, trapped in the mud of ambitions, defeated by wrong decisions, caught in the dogma of the society.

To the days we take courage to embrace the struggle, take risks and walk the tightrope, past the hardships, towards the light, no matter how narrow the road to the goal appears to be.

To the days, when things fall into place, we are euphoric again, fall in love, win over hearts, look at the bigger picture as we laugh at ourselves with our loved ones for being so lost at one point!

To the amazing people I met when I quit my job to pursue my dream and the direction they gave to my life.

To the days I have spent on the open road across India and Europe to get the inspiration for this story.

To the passion for storytelling, I have had since the earliest days in my memory, and to my relentless quest to inspire people to pursue their dreams and live life on their terms.

To the labourers I looked at every morning from my balcony, who were employed to toil day and night at the construction site due to dearth of privilege, and taught me the importance of working hard in life.

To the stars and nature for their clarion call to look till infinity and beyond, to inspiring scientists, poets, writers, painters, musicians—practically, each one of us alike.

To my readers who made this book a bestseller.

To the love of my life, Kushal.

To Mom, Dad and Swapnil, for not abandoning me despite my unconventional career choice. My dreams would not have seen the light of day without your love.

To my in-laws, my new family, who support me as their very own daughter.

To my only living grandparent, Nanijee, for loving me unconditionally and teaching me to live life to the fullest.

To my dog Lucky whom I lost in the summer of 2014, for teaching me the meaning of love.

To my team at Penguin Random House—Milee Ashwarya, Saksham Garg, Vijesh Kumar, Prateek Agarwal, Natasha Kapur, Saloni Mital, Neha Punj, Akangksha Sarmah, who gave wings to my dream of reaching millions with my stories the moment they decided to acquire and work on my self-published books.

To the first editor of my life, Roshini, who read my books and unearthed my buried potential.

To the first agent of my life, Sahil, who worked day and night to make my art commercially viable and stand out at the same time.

To my selfless and hustler manager, Vivek, who took care of all the other things so I could focus more on my creative work.

To Pushkar Singh, who gave an added dimension to my story through the enthralling cover illustrations.

To my friends and cousins who stick with me through thick and thin.

To my fans from the social media community who encourage me to do more. #SCFamily, #stutichangle is growing every day, pushing me to work harder.

To the Starbucks trio, Awatar, Vikas and Vikram, for being by my side through the ups and downs while writing this book.

To the board in Starbucks, where I completed this novel, that read, 'Extraordinary things come from tiny beans.'